Aubrey McFadden Is Never Getting Married

"Georgia Beers has become a household name in the world of LGBTQ+ romance novels, and her latest work, *Aubrey McFadden Is Never Getting Married*, proves she is worthy of the attention. With its captivating characters, engaging plot, and impactful themes, this book is a pure delight to read. Its enemies-to-lovers narrative tugs at the heart, making one hope for resolution and forgiveness between its leading ladies. Aubrey and Monica's push-and-pull dynamic is complicated and knotty, but Beers keeps it fun with her quick wit and sense of humor. The crafty banter ensures that readers have a good time."—*Women Using Words*

Playing with Matches

"*Playing with Matches* is a delightful exploration of small town life, family drama, and true love…Liz and Cori are charming characters with undeniable chemistry, and their sweet and tender small town, 'fake-dating' love story is sure to capture the attention of readers. Their journey reminds readers of the importance of love, forgiveness, family, and community, making this feel-good romance a true triumph."—*Women Using Words*

Peaches and Cream

"*Peaches and Cream* is a fresh, new spin on the classic rom-com *You've Got Mail*—except it's even better because it's all about ice cream!…[A] delicious, melt-in-your-mouth scoop of goodness. Bursting with tasty characters in a scrumptious story world, *Peaches and Cream* is simply irresistible."—*Women Using Words*

Lambda Literary Award Winner *Dance with Me*

"I admit I inherited my two left feet from my father's side of the family. Dancing is not something I enjoy, so why choose a book with dancing as the central focus and romance as the payoff? Easy. Because it's Georgia Beers, and she will let me enjoy being awkward alongside her main character. I think this is what makes her special to me as an author. While her characters might be beautiful in their own ways, I can relate to their challenges, fears and dreams. Comfort reads every time."—*Late Night Lesbian Reads*

Camp Lost and Found

"I really like when Beers writes about winter and snow and hot chocolate. She makes heartache feel cosy and surmountable. *Camp Lost and Found* made me smile a lot, laugh at times, tear up more often than I care to share. If you're looking for a heartwarming story to keep the cold weather at bay, I'd recommend you give it a chance."—*Jude in the Stars*

Cherry on Top

"*Cherry on Top* is another wonderful story from one of the greatest writers in sapphic fiction…This is more than a romance with two incredibly charming and wonderful characters. It is a reminder that you shouldn't have to compromise who you are to fit into a box that society wants to put you into. Georgia Beers once again creates a couple with wonderful chemistry who will warm your heart."—*Sapphic Book Review*

The Secret Poet

"[O]ne of the author's best works and one of the best romances I've read recently…I was so invested in [Morgan and Zoe] I read the book in one sitting."—*Melina Bickard, Librarian, Waterloo Library (UK)*

On the Rocks

"This book made me so happy! And kept me awake way too late."—*Jude in the Stars*

Hopeless Romantic

"Thank you, Georgia Beers, for this unabashed paean to the pleasure of escaping into romantic comedies...If you want to have a big smile plastered on your face as you read a romance novel, do not hesitate to pick up this one!"—*The Rainbow Bookworm*

Flavor of the Month

"Beers whips up a sweet lesbian romance...brimming with mouthwatering descriptions of foodie indulgences...Both women are well-intentioned and endearing, and it's easy to root for their inevitable reconciliation. But once the couple rediscover their natural ease with one another, Beers throws a challenging emotional hurdle in their path, forcing them to fight through tragedy to earn their happy ending."—*Publishers Weekly*

Fear of Falling

"Enough tension and drama for us to wonder if this can work out—and enough heat to keep the pages turning. I will definitely recommend this to others—Georgia Beers continues to go from strength to strength."—*Evan Blood, Bookseller (Angus & Robertson, Australia)*

One Walk in Winter

"A sweet story to pair with the holidays. There are plenty of 'moment's in this book that make the heart soar. Just what I like in a romance. Situations where sparks fly, hearts fill, and tears fall. This book shined with cute fairy trails and swoon-worthy Christmas gifts…REALLY nice and cozy if read in between Thanksgiving and Christmas. Covered in blankets. By a fire."—*Bookvark*

The Do-Over

"You can count on Beers to give you a quality well-paced book each and every time."—*The Romantic Reader Blog*

"*The Do-Over* is a shining example of the brilliance of Georgia Beers as a contemporary romance author."—*Rainbow Reflections*

The Shape of You

The Shape of You "catches you right in the feels and does not let go. It is a must for every person out there who has struggled with self-esteem, questioned their judgment, and settled for a less than perfect but safe lover. If you've ever been convinced you have to trade passion for emotional safety, this book is for you."—*Writing While Distracted*

"I know I always say this about Georgia Beers's books, but there is no one that writes first kisses like her. They are hot, steamy and all too much!"—*Les Rêveur*

Calendar Girl

"A sweet, sweet romcom of a story…*Calendar Girl* is a nice read, which you may find yourself returning to when you want a hot-chocolate-and-warm-comfort-hug in your life."—*Best Lesbian Erotica*

Blend

"You know a book is good, first, when you don't want to put it down. Second, you know it's damn good when you're reading it and thinking, I'm totally going to read this one again. Great read and absolutely a 5-star romance."—*The Romantic Reader Blog*

"This is a lovely romantic story with relatable characters that have depth and chemistry. A charming easy story that kept me reading until the end. Very enjoyable."—*Kat Adams, Bookseller, QBD (Australia)*

Right Here, Right Now

"[A] successful and entertaining queer romance novel. The main characters are appealing, and the situations they deal with are realistic and well-managed. I would recommend this book to anyone who enjoys a good queer romance novel, and particularly one grounded in real world situations."—*Books at the End of the Alphabet*

"[A]n engaging odd-couple romance. Beers creates a romance of gentle humor that allows no-nonsense Lacey to relax and easygoing Alicia to find a trusting heart."—*RT Book Reviews*

Lambda Literary Award Winner *Fresh Tracks*

"[T]he focus switches each chapter to a different character, allowing for a measured pace and deep, sincere exploration of each protagonist's thoughts. Beers gives a welcome expansion to the romance genre with her clear, sympathetic writing." —*Curve magazine*

Lambda Literary Award Finalist *Finding Home*

"Georgia Beers has proven in her popular novels such as *Too Close to Touch* and *Fresh Tracks* that she has a special way of building romance with suspense that puts the reader on the edge of their seat. *Finding Home*, though more character driven than suspense, will equally keep the reader engaged at each page turn with its sweet romance."—*Lambda Literary Review*

Mine

"Beers does a fine job of capturing the essence of grief in an authentic way. *Mine* is touching, life-affirming, and sweet."
—*Lesbian News Book Review*

Too Close to Touch

"This is such a well-written book. The pacing is perfect, the romance is great, the character work strong, and damn, but is the sex writing ever fantastic."—*The Lesbian Review*

"In her third novel, Georgia Beers delivers an immensely satisfying story. Beers knows how to generate sexual tension so taut it could be cut with a knife...Beers weaves a tale of yearning, love, lust, and conflict resolution. She has constructed a believable plot, with strong characters in a charming setting."—*Just About Write*

By the Author

Visit us at www.boldstrokesbooks.com

THIS CHRISTMAS

by

Georgia Beers

2024

ISBN 13: 978-1-63679-729-8

THIS TRADE PAPERBACK ORIGINAL IS PUBLISHED BY
BOLD STROKES BOOKS, INC.
P.O. BOX 249
VALLEY FALLS, NY 12185

FIRST EDITION: NOVEMBER 2024

CREDITS
EDITOR: RUTH STERNGLANTZ
PRODUCTION DESIGN: STACIA SEAMAN
COVER DESIGN BY INKSPIRAL DESIGN

Acknowledgments

Ah, Christmas.

I love the joy, the celebration, and how the season seems to make everybody just a little bit kinder. I haven't written a holiday novel since *Snow Globe* many, many years ago, so I thought I was due. Christmas is also the perfect time for romance to blossom. That's why Hallmark Christmas movies are so beloved. The season puts you in just the right mood for love, and that's what I wanted to convey in *This Christmas*—that it doesn't matter if you screwed up or if you chose poorly and made the wrong decision...Christmas is the season to fix it! Everybody's a little softer, so that apology or reattempt or first step toward somebody is more likely to get the desired result. Just ask Keegan Duffy, as she spends the book trying to figure out how to change the mistake she made last year regarding Sammi Sorenson. Christmas seems to be exactly the right time to fix things. Throw in some quirky family, a whole bunch of dogs, all kinds of holiday traditions, and a return to Junebug Farms, and you have *This Christmas*. I hope you enjoy reading it as much as I enjoyed writing it. Happy holidays!

On to the thank-yous:

I think I've finally settled into this new chapter of my life (see what I did there?), and it feels good. I'm so grateful for my unconventional family, as well as the friends who've stuck by me and supported me during such a strange transition and all the adjustment time. Thank you to that small group. You, your understanding, and your encouragement mean more than you know.

I'd be remiss if I didn't mention my dog and cat, Archie and Emmett. Some people say "It's just a dog" or "It's just a cat," but they are so much more than that to me. They are my babies. I love them to bits. I recently took a long trip and was away from them for fifteen days. I missed them so much it made my chest ache, and it made me realize just how important they are to my daily life and my mental health. They are a source of quiet love and support throughout my workdays, my weekends, and my nights, and I'm so glad they're with me. (They made the return to Junebug Farms in this book even sweeter, as they are both rescues.)

As always, thank you to all the people at Bold Strokes Books who keep the wheels turning and the books churning out. I'm so lucky to have such a supportive publisher, and I am grateful every day for how smooth the process of publishing my books seems to be. I have heard so many horror stories, so I know how lucky I am.

And last, but never, ever least: thank you to my readers, my patrons, and everybody who follows me, hits a like on my posts, sends me email, joins my Patreon page, messages, DMs…you are the ones who keep me going. This is a crazy, unpredictable, very solitary career I have, and hearing from readers and supporters that they have enjoyed my work makes it all worthwhile. So, thank you from the bottom of my very, very grateful heart. You keep reading, and I'll keep writing.

To everybody who decorates for the holidays early.
Don't listen to the naysayers.
Put up that tree!

PROLOGUE

It's too much...

The words ran through Keegan's head as if somebody was sitting inside her skull shouting them at her. It was too good, but too much, too soon, overwhelming...Sammi's mouth was on hers, and Sammi's hands were on her body, and Keegan was pretty sure she was on fire, had simply ignited, and was now being consumed by flames so hot they were blue, and it was all just too much.

"God." She gave Sammi a gentle push, but she didn't stop, and Keegan shoved at her harder. "Stop. Please. Stop."

The surprise on Sammi's face was almost comical, it was so clear. She pulled back and sat up, eyes wide, lips swollen, breasts heaving. "What? Why? Did I hurt you?"

"No. No." Keegan slid herself out from under Sammi and pushed off the couch. Her shirt hung open, and she buttoned it as quickly as her shaking hands would allow.

"Keegan. Seriously. What is it?" Sammi blinked at her, still on her knees on the couch. "Talk to me."

"It's...I don't know. I just, I can't. It's too..." God, she was so fucking embarrassed right now, but aside from that, the only thing she felt in that moment was relief. Her anxiety was slowly easing, and her panic had stopped climbing. "Could we..." She groaned, made a sound of confused frustration. "God, could we just never talk about this again? Go back to being friends for now? Please." She shook her head as Sammi's face fell. Like, literally, the smile seemed to fall right off her face, leaving only sad confusion. "I'm sorry. I just need to—I have to go. I'm sorry. I'm so sorry."

She left Sammi there. Beautiful Sammi. Sweet Sammi. Sammi who she had major, *major* feelings for, feelings that were swamping her already. No. No, she couldn't do it. Not again. She had to go home because it was all too much, too fast, and she'd vowed never to do that again. Not after last time.

Her eyes burned with tears as she drove, and not for the first time, she cursed her tender heart and her stubborn brain. Jumping in headfirst only got her hurt. She knew this from experience. And yet, there she'd been, at Sammi's house, on her back on the couch, Sammi above her, while she dived right off the diving board and into the pool of emotion and confusion and potential heartbreak.

No. No, it was better this way. Sammi didn't deserve her waffling, her uncertainty. God, her outright fear and paranoia. No. She'd done the right thing. She was sure of it.

She glanced at her own eyes in the rearview mirror. They looked haunted. Sad. And as she watched, they filled with tears, and she sniffled.

"It'll be okay," she whispered into the empty car. "It'll be okay." Sammi would probably need some time away from her, some space to lick her wounds, and then they'd be able to go back to being the good friends they had been. That's the way it needed to be. That's what would be best. Just a little time. That's all she'd need.

A big breath in, and then she let it out slowly, starting to feel the tiniest bit better. She wiped under her eyes, then pulled a tissue from her pocket and blew her nose.

"It'll be okay."

She'd done the right thing.

Hadn't she?

CHAPTER ONE

Eleven months later

Was there any problem in life that couldn't be made at least a teensy bit better with Mexican food and a margarita? Keegan Duffy didn't think so. And the way her muscles relaxed and her step grew light as she opened the door to Mama Maria's and found herself bathed in the warmth and aromas of melted cheese, simmering mole, and spicy meat only proved her theory.

Before the hostess could approach her, she caught a wave from across the restaurant. Sammi.

"Well, aren't you a lovely sight for my sore eyes?" Sammi stood as Keegan approached, then held out her arms for a firm hug. Sammi was an excellent hugger. Keegan had always thought so. None of that quick touch of shoulders and pat-pat on the back. No way. Sammi *hugged* you. She wrapped you up tight and squeezed. Held on. Made you feel like you mattered, like hugging you properly was important to her.

"Why are your eyes sore?" Keegan asked with a grin as she sat across from Sammi at the round table for two. "Are people forgetting to floss again?"

"People always forget to floss."

"Those are the ones that keep you in business."

The waitress arrived with two margaritas before Keegan had ordered. She glanced at Sammi. "Bless you."

"Didn't want you to have to wait."

The waitress said she'd give them a few minutes and headed off to another table.

Sammi lifted her glass. "It's good to see you, my friend."

Keegan touched her glass to Sammi's. "Right back atcha."

Half an hour later, they were enjoying delicious meals and a second margarita each, laughing like they always did together.

"You know," Sammi said, her deep, rich dark eyes dancing in the dim restaurant lighting. "I love that we can go for weeks—or even, I think it's been months this time—and not miss a beat. We pick right back up." Her cheeks held a slight flush when she was happy, something Keegan had always found endearing.

"Same." She sipped. "I mean, we do text, thank God."

"Yeah, true, but I've gotten really bad at texting back. And besides, it's not the same as actually seeing your face." The flush deepened. "When *was* the last time we got together?" Sammi scrunched up her face, clearly racking her brain. "I can't remember."

"I think...end of summer?" Keegan feigned uncertainty, but she knew exactly when they'd last met. July thirteenth. She knew because she'd gone on her first date with Jules on the fourteenth. But Sammi didn't know that. Yet.

"Too long," Sammi said. "Too long, I say." She dunked a chip into the queso, took a bite, then asked, "So? What's new? How are the kids? Stir-crazy in anticipation of Halloween?"

"Oh my God, they're absurd. Totally absurd." Teaching kindergarten had been her dream job since she was fourteen years old. She was now in her tenth year of teaching and her fifth year of teaching kindergarten, and every day, she wondered how it was that she'd gotten so lucky. "If somebody's little head just exploded tomorrow during story time, I wouldn't be even a tiny bit surprised." She took a bite of enchilada, then pointed her fork at Sammi. "And how is your mom? Your grandma? Are they still spying on your every move?"

"Always." Sammi's laugh was pretty. Musical, like tinkling wind chimes. The sound somehow seemed unexpected coming from Sammi. Keegan had always equated her dark hair and eyes and the tanned tone of her skin to a woman of reserve and mystery, but that delicate laugh somehow contradicted the vision. "I mean, what did I expect when I bought a house across the street from them, right?" "You also have a normal mom and a normal grandma. I could never live that close to my mother. I'd have to kill myself. Or her. It would depend on the day."

"Well, they're great. Grandma is the busiest retired person I've ever met. Between her three book clubs, her knitting circle, the Italian cooking class she's taking, her wine tastings, and the dog walking group, I don't know when she has time to sleep."

"If I could have half—no, I won't even be greedy, I'll take a quarter. If I could have a quarter of the energy your grandma has, I'd be unstoppable."

"She is something." Sammi's face beamed with pride. Keegan knew how close the two of them were, and she found herself envious, having lost her own grandmother last year. Sammi set her fork down and dabbed at her mouth with a napkin. Then she propped her chin in her hand and her elbow on the table. "What else is new? Anything?"

"Actually, yes." Keegan set her own fork down and picked up her drink, suddenly a little nervous. She took a sip, then spoke. "I've been seeing someone."

Sammi seemed to freeze for a second or two. Her expression locked. She blinked a couple times, and then her face shifted into a smile. A forced one, it seemed, but a smile. "Oh?"

Keegan nodded.

"For how long? How'd you meet?" Sammi picked her fork back up and poked at her rice and beans, as if that singular focus she'd had on Keegan a few minutes ago had been shoved to the side.

"Online. Isn't that where everybody meets these days?" A laugh, and it was overly loud, and oh God, she sounded so stupid. "A couple months." Three and a half, actually, but she didn't say that.

"Great. That's awesome." Sammi took a bite, then seemed like she wished she hadn't. "What does she do?"

"She works for a remodeling company. She's a salesperson. Tile and flooring and new kitchens and stuff."

"Great. That's awesome."

"What about you?"

"What about me?"

"Are you dating? Looking to date?" Keegan worked hard to right the conversation that had somehow gotten derailed.

Sammi lifted one shoulder. "I don't have a ton of time. One of these days, maybe." Again, she smiled. Again, it didn't quite reach her eyes.

Okay, it was clearly time for a subject change. Keegan had known it was going to be weird to talk to Sammi about dating somebody—for *both* of them—but they needed to get past that horrible night. They couldn't live in its shadow forever. "Done any volunteering at Junebug Farms lately? Barktoberfest is coming up."

At the mention of the no-kill animal shelter that was near and dear to both their hearts, Sammi seemed to relax a bit. The clouds in her dark eyes cleared somewhat, and this smile, though soft and slight, was the real deal. "Not in a while, but I'm definitely planning to go to that. You?"

"Oh, absolutely. Wouldn't miss it." She finished her margarita. "The chances of us seeing each other again soon are looking pretty good. Yeah?"

"Yeah." The smile grew. Thank God. Keegan didn't like seeing Sammi uncertain or sad or in any kind of state that wasn't happiness. They steered the conversation into much safer waters as they split an order of flan. By the time they finished the last bite, they were laughing again, something that had always come easy to the two of them.

They fought over the bill, but Sammi won, as she so often did, using her standard *teachers get paid squat* argument that Keegan couldn't really stand up against, because duh. It was the truth. Once outside, they hovered on the sidewalk. Keegan had walked, her apartment literally three blocks away.

"You okay to drive?" she asked Sammi as she walked her to her car.

"Promise." They hugged, and this time Sammi's hug was

slightly less than her usual vigorous hug but was still more solid than almost anybody else's, and Keegan held on tight.

"Text me when you get home," she said, pointing at Sammi.

Sammi pointed back. "Yes, ma'am."

Keegan stood to the side as Sammi started her car, backed out, and gave her a wave before driving away. For reasons she didn't want to dwell on, a bit of a gray cloud seemed to drift up overhead and hang out there, a melancholy that settled over her.

She inhaled a deep lungful of the October night air, crisp and cool. Not cold yet, but definitely not warm. The scent of fall was in that inhale—crushed leaves and damp earth and apples—and she held it in for an extra couple of seconds, just to absorb the impending season.

Long after Sammi's taillights had disappeared, Keegan stared after them. That had gone about how she thought it would go, but she still felt an ache somewhere deep in her soul. She blew out a breath in resignation, and finally, she turned and began her short stroll home.

❖

Sammi's grandmother was eighty years old, but you'd never know it if you followed her around for a day. She was more active than most middle-aged people Sammi knew, and her social calendar was stuffed full of events and clubs and meetings. That's why it didn't faze Sammi at all when she headed outside on Thursday morning to go to work and saw her grandma across the street, raking leaves in her front lawn.

It was barely seven thirty.

She scooted across the cul-de-sac. "Hey, Grams. Leaves couldn't wait until actual daylight?" she teased.

Her grandmother grinned as she shot a quick glance at the sky, which was certainly light. "Funny." She tilted her head so Sammi could kiss her cheek. "Just felt like getting in some movement this morning. It's so glorious out." She stood with both hands clasped on the rake handle, closed her eyes, and inhaled deeply through her nose. "Smell that?"

Sammi could. "Smells like fall. Your favorite." She reached for the rake. "Can I help? I have a little time."

Her grandmother playfully slapped her hands away as Sammi laughed. "Not in your work clothes. No, I got this." She tapped a finger against her chest. "Good for my heart."

"Heading to Junebug Farms today?" It was Thursday, after all, and that was one of her dog-walking days.

"Yup. Gotta get ready for Barktoberfest. You're coming, right?" A nod. "Absolutely."

"Oh! I forgot about your dinner last night. How did it go? How's Keegan?" Her grandmother had always had a soft spot for Keegan. From the moment they'd first met—at Junebug Farms, coincidentally, at one of their events—she'd been trying to play matchmaker. Didn't matter how many times Sammi asked her to stop, her grandmother was certain she knew best and that Sammi and Keegan made a fabulous couple. "You two are *M-F-E-O*, as my goddess of all television, Shonda Rhimes, would say," she'd told Sammi more than once.

I mean, she's not wrong, except...

"She's good. Really good. Seeing somebody now, I guess." Did that come off light and casual? 'Cause that's what she was trying for.

"Oh." Her grandmother was clearly disappointed by this news, and Sammi wasn't surprised. "Oh, I see." She looked like she wanted to say more, and Sammi was relieved when the front door opened and her mother appeared.

"Hi, sweetie," she said, wrapping her arms around herself in her light joggers and long-sleeve T-shirt.

"Hey, Mom."

"Chilly."

"Grandma doesn't think so."

"That's because she's going senile and doesn't know any better." Her mother shot a quick grin at her grandmother. This was their relationship. They teased mercilessly. They loved unconditionally. Sammi's mother had moved in after Sammi's father had passed away to help her grandma with the grief of losing her son. Turned out, her mom needed just as much help with the grief of losing her husband, and she ended up never leaving. Then Sammi bought the house across the cul-de-sac. They all looked out for each other, and Sammi wouldn't have it any other way.

"Don't think I won't cut you right out of my will," her grandmother said now in feigned seriousness. "I'll leave everything to my granddaughter here and skip right over your skinny ass."

"All I hear is blah, blah, blah," Sammi's mother said, opening and closing her hand like a puppet, as Sammi shook her head and laughed softly. These women. They were her rocks. They drove her a little batty at times, but she loved them fiercely.

"I gotta get to work," she said and bent to kiss her mom on the cheek. She pointed at her grandma. "Don't you overdo it, understand?"

Her grandmother turned to her mother and lowered her voice. "She's really gotten bossy in her old age."

"I know, right?" her mother said.

"You two are hilarious," Sammi tossed over her shoulder as she headed back across the circle. "Bye."

Half an hour later, she was seated at her desk in her office. Her schedule was pretty full today, which was good. Made the day go by faster.

She'd worked hard on her practice. When she'd finished her degree, her first job had been at a dental clinic with six other dentists. And it was fine. There were a couple of older dentists who'd been good about teaching, and she'd learned a lot. But she didn't love the extra rules or the answering to other people, and she didn't love being the lowest rung on the ladder. After two years at the clinic, she made a decision. She stayed for another eighteen months, learned as much as she possibly could stuff into her brain, and she saved every last cent she had. And then finally, two years ago at the ripe old age of thirty-two, she'd opened her own practice.

It had been hard. Exhausting. There had been times where she'd wondered why the hell she ever thought answering to somebody else wasn't worse than making nine million decisions all on her own, seemingly every single day. But she'd slogged through. She'd advertised. She'd done free clinics for the underserved and uninsured. Anything to get her name out there. She worked her damn ass off for the past two years, and it was finally paying off.

She sat back in her chair now—her comfy, ergonomically correct chair that she'd splurged and spent nearly a thousand dollars on because she knew how much time she'd spend sitting in it—and took in her office. She did that every now and then. It was a deep slate blue color with ivory trim. Very classy. Elegant. The floor was a laminate that looked like hardwood, but she'd added a large, round area rug to warm it up. Her desk was cherry, rich and deep. Her diplomas hung on the wall—copies were hanging in a couple of the patient rooms—as did a few paintings she'd been drawn to. Nothing fancy, just some framed prints from Michael's, but they brought some life to the room. One was a nighttime cityscape of Manhattan. The other was a painting of a café in the summer, three small tables lined up on a sidewalk, customers eating desserts and sipping wine.

Across the room on the other wall, though, was her favorite. A gift from her grandmother, it was her late grandfather's framed print of *Dogs Playing Poker*. The day she opened her practice, her grandma had come by with it.

"Your grandpa had this hanging in his office at the insurance company for almost forty years, and he used to tell me how it made him smile on even the worst days." She'd held it out to Sammi. "I know he'd want you to have it."

She hadn't been wrong—even now, Sammi sat at her desk and grinned at the antics of the card-playing canines. Funny how something so silly could make her happy in the moment.

A tiny chime from her phone told her a text had come through, and she sat up to grab it from her desk. It was Keegan, and Sammi smiled automatically.

Thanks for dinner and an amazing time last night...next time, I buy!

A knock on her doorframe yanked her attention from the phone. Michelle, one of her hygienists. "Dr. Sammi? We're ready for you in exam one."

With a nod, she set the phone back down. She'd have to answer later.

Her first patient was Carter Jackson, a five-year-old whose family was new to the area.

"Hey, Carter," she said as she entered the room. "I'm Dr. Sammi. Michelle said you did great today, that you were super brave and not scared at all."

He shook his head. His mother sat in a chair in the corner, smiling with clear pride, and gave her a nod.

Sammi pointed at his Avengers shirt. "Which one's your favorite? I'm kinda partial to Iron Man myself."

"I like Thor," Carter said, his voice quiet as he followed her with his eyes as if he didn't quite trust her yet. After all, he'd spent the past forty-five minutes getting used to Michelle. Now, he had to deal with her too?

"Thor is definitely cool. I wish I had that hammer, don't you?" This nod was a bit more enthusiastic, so she asked him to open, and she checked everything out. "You're new in town, huh? Are you in kindergarten?" She paused her exam as he nodded again.

"He loves his teacher, Miss Duffy," his mother said from the corner. "Don't you, kiddo?"

This time, a slight blush came along with his nod, and Sammi felt her heart give a little kick. "Do you know that Miss Duffy is a good friend of mine?" Carter's eyes went wide in disbelief. "I know. What are the chances, right? But Northwood's a big little city. When you go back to school, you tell her Dr. Sammi said hi, okay?" *We obviously have a crush on the same girl*, she almost added but caught it just in time.

Between dinner last night, the text this morning, and young Carter Jackson, the Universe didn't seem like it was about to let her stop thinking about Keegan. Not just yet...

❖

Keegan set her phone back down on her desk. Sammi hadn't responded yet, and that was okay. She would. Keegan knew her pretty well, and even if she was angry or frustrated or whatever, she always texted back. Hearing about Jules hadn't been easy for her, that had been clear last night, so maybe she just needed a little time before she answered Keegan's text.

She inhaled deeply through her nose, then let it out her mouth. This was her favorite time of the workday, the first fifteen or twenty minutes alone in her classroom before the kids arrived. Everything was neat. The scents of construction paper and crayons hung in the air. The magnets were tidy, the toys all put away, the books lined up on the shelves, just waiting for story time. And then the kids would arrive in a flurry of sound and running footsteps and excitement, and she could hardly wait for them to get settled before she said good morning and told them what their plan was for today. Their open minds. Their innocent smiles. Their enthusiastic anticipation. She had no words for how much she loved it all.

Some days, she couldn't believe this was her life. She'd wanted to be a teacher since she was a child. Every Christmas, her parents gave her something teacher related, until she'd had an entire makeshift classroom in the basement. She'd spent hours down there teaching all her dolls the alphabet and numbers and colors. She smiled now, thinking about how her parents likely still had some of that stuff somewhere on their property. And now, here she was, a bona fide kindergarten teacher, and she wouldn't have it any other way.

The bell rang and then the sound of footsteps pounded through the halls. The older kids—the second and third and fourth graders— always seemed to run, sprinting to their classrooms. Kindergarteners were a bit more subtle, at least for a bit longer. School had only been in session for six weeks, and it still felt a bit new and uncertain to some of her kids.

They began filing in. She didn't have desks in her classroom, she had tables, and she didn't assign seats, but as had happened every year since she'd started teaching this grade, kids tended to sit in the same seat each day. It was a comfort thing, a familiar touchstone in what was still a somewhat unfamiliar setting.

"Good morning, Tasha," she said to the first child through the door. Tasha smiled shyly as she unzipped her jacket and hung it on the hook above the little cubby with her name on it in purple construction-paper letters. Next came Jordie, then Michael, then Devon, then Alex the girl, followed by Alex the boy. Keegan sat and smiled and greeted each child. The sound volume in the room grew exponentially as the kids began to chat with their friends. A couple of the boys wrestled and laughed. A group of four little girls all sat at one table and were chatting about hair, what accessories they liked best, which color of barrette was the favorite. Within about eight minutes, her entire class was present.

She glanced at her phone. Still blank. She slid it into her purse, which she then tucked into the bottom drawer of her desk. She stood up and cleared her throat.

"Good morning, class."

"Good morning, Miss Duffy," they said back in unison.

CHAPTER TWO

Junebug Farms no-kill animal shelter was one of Mia Sorenson's favorite places in the whole wide world. She was a lover of animals—especially dogs—but her late husband had been severely allergic. So her son, Kevin, had never been able to have a dog growing up, much to his and Mia's grave disappointment. To make up for it, though, she had gotten him familiar with the shelter, and they'd volunteered all the time, walking the dogs, helping with fundraising—Kevin had even worked there part-time when he'd been going to the local community college. And long after Mia had lost both her husband and her son, she'd continued to show up at Junebug Farms because the dogs needed to see friendly faces. That's how she looked at it. Spending your days in a small kennel had to be hard, especially for the ones who'd been abandoned by their families. Mia struggled with that scenario and always did her best to lavish those dogs with a little extra love.

That Saturday was brisk. The weather had gone from pleasantly cool to much closer to cold, a typical fall day in upstate New York. The sky was a dull gray, and there was a mist in the air that seemed almost like it was hanging there, rather than actually falling to the ground. They were going to have to wipe down the dogs after they walked.

She pulled into the parking lot and immediately saw Francie and Angelo walking together toward the front door. Beth was likely inside because she was always early. Carmen was likely not here yet because she was always late. Mia gathered her purse and bag and headed inside.

The cacophony of endless barking was something she'd never get used to. It was the first thing that hit when you walked through the front doors of Junebug Farms, even though the dogs were off in their own wing. But it was fall now, and the shelter was almost filled to capacity—never a good thing for an animal shelter. The endless barking and the jab to her heart. Those were the things she'd never get used to. While she was endlessly grateful that Junebug was no-kill, it didn't make it any easier to see row after row of abandoned dogs sitting behind cage doors, wanting nothing more than some attention and to be loved.

There were days when it broke her heart.

But Mia Sorenson was also grateful for those days, because they reminded her that she was alive. At eighty years old, she needed as many of those reminders as she could get, and if they came from dogs rather than people, so be it.

She waved to the two women behind the horseshoe-shaped front desk. They waved back because she was a fixture here, and she continued on to the volunteer break room toward the back of the lobby.

"Good morning, friends," she said in a cheerful, singsong voice. "It's a beautiful day."

Angelo's laugh was big and deep and throaty, which always came as a surprise to Mia, given that he was not a big man at all. "You say that every day, Mia," he said, affection lining his tone.

"Not sure if you noticed," Francie added, "but it's raining out. And it's cold."

Leave it to Francie to pick out all the negatives. Mia managed not to roll her eyes. "I say it every day because it's true. Every day I wake up is a beautiful day."

Angelo nodded, and they were saved from any more debate over whether or not the day was beautiful by Beth's arrival.

"Happy Saturday, my walking friends," she said, almost as cheerful as Mia had been. Mia loved that about her. "I come bearing gifts." She held up a box from Dunkin'.

"Ah, sustenance," Angelo said, taking the box from her and setting it on the round table in the middle of the break room. He wasted no time opening it and helping himself to the raspberry jelly doughnut, which they all knew was his favorite, and whoever turn it was to bring the doughnuts knew to grab at least two of that variety.

"Good morning to my favorite walkers."

Mia turned to meet the smiling face of Lisa, the adoption and intake manager at Junebug. She was tall and pretty with short, light hair and serious eyes, and today, there seemed to be a shadow of something else as well. Worry? Concern? Mia wasn't sure.

"What are you doing here on a Saturday, Lisa?" Mia asked.

"Big emergency intake last night," Lisa said, and her serious expression grew even more so. "Everybody was called in. Hoarding situation. We've got some very scared pups back there, so I'm hoping you guys can give them some extra attention and love. Baths, walks, hugs, whatever you can spare."

Something Mia admired about Lisa was that she never seemed to grow cold or unfeeling around the animals. Mia knew that she'd been doing this job for a long time, and it would make sense if she'd become numb or burned out. But she wasn't. Yes, she was a generally serious person, but Mia had also seen her eyes filled with unshed tears over a situation or a particular animal that touched her heart. All of Junebug's employees were like that.

"Attention and love are why we're here," Mia said, forcing extra cheer into her tone. "Right, guys?"

The others nodded, their expressions taking on a mix of Lisa's seriousness and Mia's exuberance.

For the next couple of hours, they walked. They'd each choose a dog, leash them up, and take them for a little jaunt around the Junebug grounds, which were sizable. The mist had let up, but the chill had also increased, and Mia pulled her coat more tightly around herself as she walked a cute little Pomeranian mix, his curly tail swishing back and forth as he moved along.

The grounds of Junebug Farms were surprisingly large. The main building that housed the dogs and cats up for adoption wasn't the only one and they weren't the only animals. To the right of the main building was a smaller goat house, which, as the name implied, housed goats. It was also set up so visitors could feed and pet them if they wanted. To the left of the main building, a few hundred yards away, was the barn. There lived the farm animals that had been rescued or surrendered. Horses of all sizes, donkeys, pigs, cows, you name it, Junebug had at least a couple. Seeing the sadness on the faces of those animals—the pigs and cows especially—had been the catalyst for Mia to stop eating meat, nearly forty years ago now. Many of her friends didn't get it. They thought she was silly because *People have always eaten meat!*, or they mistakenly thought the end of the animal meat industry would cripple the whole of the American economy, so she didn't talk about it. She never pushed her plant-based views on other people. She just did what felt right for her, and she was much happier that way. There was simply no way she could pet a cow—one of the gentlest creatures she'd ever met—look into its eyes, and then go order a burger. No way.

She and her Pomeranian walked along with Angelo and his beagle mix. "This guy could use some leash walking lessons," he muttered as the beagle left absolutely zero slack in the leash.

Mia laughed softly. "Wanna switch?"

"Nah." Angelo smiled his thanks at her. "He's just excited to be out of his kennel."

He was right, Mia knew. "Wouldn't you be?"

"Absolutely, I would."

They followed the trail toward the barn while Beth and her German shepherd had gone the opposite direction, and Francie and Carmen—who'd finally showed up—took their walkers across the street to the nature trail. Angelo was her favorite walking companion of the bunch, though she loved them all.

"So? How are you? Doing all right?"

Angelo nodded, his soft blue eyes gazing off into the distance. "Yeah. I'm okay. The holidays are coming. That's always hard."

Mia nodded, remembering her first few holidays after her husband Bob had passed, then again years later when she'd lost Kevin. "They do get easier. They're never *easy*, but they do get easier."

"That's what people keep telling me." They stopped so the beagle could sniff a bush. "It'll be two years in November that Tim's been gone. Honestly, Mia, it feels like yesterday and also feels like forever, and I'm not sure how that's possible."

"Oh, I so understand that, and I've got no explanation." She smiled at him, hoping to soften his suffering a bit. "How long were you together again?"

"Twenty-seven years."

"Ah. Long time. Bob and I made it to our fortieth anniversary before he passed."

"Oh wow. I'm sorry." They followed the trail around the barn until they were headed back in the direction they'd come.

"Thank you. It took a while, but I finally got to a point where, instead of being angry that we didn't have more time together, I'm grateful to have had the time we did."

Angelo nodded, and Mia saw his throat move once, twice, and knew a subject change was in order.

"What about a dog? Or a cat? Have you thought of that? Adopting something to keep you company?"

There was a smile. Finally! Angelo grinned at her. "I actually have been thinking about that. Tim and I lost both our cats just before he got sick. And then it was just too much to think about bringing another pet into the house with all he was going through."

"Sure."

"But now…I might be ready."

Mia reached out and stroked a hand down his arm as she smiled up at him. "That's terrific, Ang."

"God knows I could use something to focus on. Maybe get me off the couch." He glanced at her. "Hey, how come you don't have a pet?"

Mia sighed as they approached the back of the main building. "I am honestly so busy." She shook her head. "I'd love a dog. I really would. But I am out almost every night of the week. I'd adopt a dog just to leave him cooped up in my house, which isn't fair."

Angelo gave her a skeptical look, and it made her laugh.

"I know, I know."

"You should think about it," he said as he held the door for her. "Any pet would be lucky to have you. And you live with your daughter-in-law, right? Wouldn't she be able to help?"

Their conversation was interrupted by Beth, who was headed back into the building at the same time they were. "Well, this girl is a dream," she said, referring to the German shepherd she'd walked. "What a sweetheart." Unlike Angelo or Mia, Beth had already adopted three dogs over the past two years they'd all been walking together.

"Gonna add her to your crew?" Mia asked with a knowing grin.

"Do not tempt me, ma'am," Beth said on a laugh.

"You have the space," Mia reminded her, referring to Beth's fifteen acres she shared with her husband.

"What did I just say about tempting me? My husband would kill me." But there was a sparkle in her eye, and they all knew her husband would be just fine. He always was.

Mia wanted to use the restroom before taking another dog out for a walk, so she headed down the hall. On the way, she passed Jessica Barstow's office. Jessica had inherited Junebug Farms from her grandmother, and she took great pride in the shelter, in its purpose, its mission, its residents. Mia had known her since Jessica's grandmother had run things and Jessica was just a teenager. Then Jessica took over and Mia kept coming, and despite Jessica being just a little bit older than Sammi, they'd hit it off and become instant friends. Which was why Mia could tell just by taking a quick glance into the office at Jessica that something was wrong. Normally a woman of action, a person who rarely stopped moving once she was inside the building, Jessica instead sat at her desk staring off into space, nibbling on her bottom lip.

Taking a detour from her trip to the restroom, Mia stopped at Jessica's door and rapped on the frame. "Knock, knock."

The sound seemed to startle Jessica, judging by the way she flinched slightly. When she met Mia's gaze, she smiled. "Hey, Mia. How are you?"

"Better than you, apparently. Everything okay?"

Jessica furrowed her brow and looked like she was trying hard to pretend to be surprised by Mia's words. "What do you mean? Everything's fine."

Mia arched an eyebrow and tipped her head to the side. She didn't have to wait long.

Jessica sighed. "I hate that you can read me so well."

"I'll take that as a compliment." Mia stepped into the office. "Everything okay with Sydney?"

"She's great. Deserves a wife who doesn't work quite so much, but..."

"She knew what she was getting into when she married you," Mia finished, smiling.

"She did." Jessica held Mia's gaze for a long moment before sighing again. "We lost some state funding. Like, a lot of it."

"Oh no."

"I mean, it's not the end of the world, but we're gonna need to do an extra fundraising campaign or two. Or seven. Ugh."

"Then that's what you do, right?"

"Yeah. I guess. Our donors are already so generous. I hate going *I know you guys give us a ton of money, but...could you give some more?*"

Mia leaned on her hands so she was a bit closer to Jessica as she spoke. "You listen to me. Nobody donates to Junebug Farms because they feel forced. Nobody. Your donors love this place, and if you need more help, those are the people you ask for it. Anybody who can help will. Happily."

"I'm sure you're right." She said it on a small sigh and didn't look all that convinced, but then she added, "We have a great fundraising expert who's helping us with some really fun ideas."

"Oh yeah? Can you tell me?"

Jessica snort-laughed. "Mia. Please. I tell you things I don't tell my wife." At Mia's feigned gasp of horror, she laughed and said, "Okay, that's not entirely true. But I would." As Mia laughed softly, she went on. "We're going to take nominations for a king and queen of the farm at Barktoberfest. People will be able to nominate their loved ones. Or themselves. Whatever. It's pretty informal. Then we're going to tally up the winners in a couple of weeks. We'll send those two on a bunch of holiday-themed errands, to some holiday events, and then put them on our Christmas parade float, always with some of our adoptable dogs. We'll post on social media and maybe get some local news coverage and"—she pressed her lips together in a thin line for a moment—"hopefully, it'll bring in some donations." She met Mia's gaze. "The shelter's been full for months now, thanks to all the people who adopted pets during the pandemic and then decided they didn't have time for them once they went back to work. We really need some help, Mia. We're struggling here."

Mia gave Jessica a smile and reassured her some more, but she spent the rest of the day worrying. Junebug Farms did so much good, and the idea of things being uncertain didn't sit well with her.

She was talking to Beth about it a little later, after the other walkers had headed home.

"These are the times I wish I was a wealthy woman," she said, as she and Beth walked along toward the barn, each of them with a shelter dog on a leash.

"Just these times?" Beth asked with a grin. "I wish that all the time."

"You know what I mean," Mia said with a smile as her dog—a Lab mix—stopped to pee on a tree. "I'd give them so much money, they'd put a wing on the main building and name it after me."

"I honestly don't know how Jessica does it." Beth's voice grew serious. "I mean, I know there are people who surrender their animals because they have no other choice. I do understand that. It's the people who are just too lazy to put in the work that I'd have a hard time with." She shook her head as they walked. "I don't know how she doesn't punch each of them right in the face. I would."

"Me too."

Mia's worry went into her evening, and it was still sitting with her when she went to bed that night. It was her curse: People, places, and things she cared about earned her worry. There wasn't much she could do, she knew that. Spread the word, volunteer her time, give money when she could. She sighed heavily as she rolled onto her side.

It just didn't seem like enough.

CHAPTER THREE

I might end up with a dog after today, you know." Shannon Duffy
was almost giddy at the possibility. "I'll just blame you, so Mom
doesn't get mad at me."

Keegan shifted her car into park and turned to her little sister.
"Please. Mom get mad at you?" She snorted to punctuate her point.
"You're the Oops Baby. You get whatever you want." She said
it lightly because that's how she meant it, and Shannon took no
offense. She never did.

"Not my fault!" Shannon called out as she exited the car. "Wow,
look at all of this cool stuff."

Barktoberfest was in full swing at Junebug Farms. Mother
Nature had been kind, gifting them a Saturday in late October that
was sunny and gorgeous rather than cold and rainy. The sky was
a bright electric blue, not a cloud to be seen. The sun shone down
warmly. Keegan had chosen leggings, a long white hoodie, and a
black puffy vest and was happy that she was going to be perfectly
comfortable.

The Junebug Farms property had been transformed since the
last time Keegan visited. When had that been? Last month? The
month before? White tent tops dotted the space on either side of
the main building—vendors selling their wares, game booths—and
at the far end of the large parking lot, several food trucks fed the
crowd. There were dogs on leashes everywhere, people having been
encouraged to bring theirs.

"God, it's been so long since I've been here," Shannon said

quietly, standing still as if trying to figure out where to go first. "You bringing your kids again this year?"

Keegan nodded. "Next month, actually. All five kindergarten classes."

A snort from Shannon. "That's a lot of small kids running around."

"It is. They handle it well here, though." Her phone pinged and she glanced down at it. A text from Jules.

Have so much fun today! Sorry I couldn't make it. Miss you! That was followed by a kissing emoji. She slid the phone back into her pocket.

"Okay, I have a plan." Keegan smiled at her little sister's words. Shannon always needed a plan, a map for tackling whatever lay in front of her. She pointed toward the food trucks. "We get food first. We're gonna need energy to make it through all these booths and go make kissy faces at the doggos inside." She pointed as she explained her logic. "Then we circle around and come back this way, hitting those tents, and that will bring us back to the food trucks again. Because we'll be hungry by then." A glance back up at her. "What do you think?"

"Solid plan. Let's do it."

They headed toward the food trucks and began at the Greek food one called Gyro Gonna Love It where they got, yes, gyros. Keegan was just biting into hers, a messy, delicious affair, when a voice tickled her senses.

"Oh man, that looks good." And there was Sammi, a big smile on her face. She wore jeans and hiking boots with a flannel shirt in purples and dark blues, a long sleeve white Henley underneath— unbuttoned enough to give Keegan an enticing view of skin. Her dark hair was pulled back into a ponytail, and a pair of sunglasses was perched on her head. When Keegan finally met her eyes, they were crinkled at the corners in a smile. "I've seen you twice in one month now. That's gotta be a record."

Keegan chewed, painfully aware of the enormous mouthful of food she was stuck dealing with. Luckily, Shannon came to the rescue by sticking out her hand.

"Hi. I'm Shannon, Keeg's little sister. And you are…?"

Sammi took Shannon's hand and shook it. "Sammi Sorenson. I guess…friend?…of your sister's."

"Oh, Sammi, right. I've heard *all* about you." Shannon said the words cryptically, and she drew out the word *all* so it had about five syllables. Sammi blanched.

Keegan chewed faster and finally swallowed. "Hey." She dabbed at her mouth with the paper napkin she'd snagged. "Amazing here, isn't it?"

Sammi recovered quickly and looked around, nodding. "They've outdone themselves, that's for sure." She lowered her voice. "My grandma said they're really hurting for donations. Lost some state funding or something."

"Oh man, that sucks." Her phone pinged and she juggled her gyro and the phone as Shannon looked over at the screen and made a sound that was less than flattering.

"Ugh. Jules." Shannon glanced up at Sammi. "Some chick she's dating. Bo-ring!"

If Keegan had had a free hand, she'd have swatted at her little sister. Instead, she had to settle for leveling a glare at her, which Shannon simply shrugged off.

"Well," Sammi said, looking suddenly uncomfortable, "I'll leave you to it. It was nice to meet you, Shannon." She turned and headed off in the direction of the main building, and Keegan watched her go, feeling a mix of things she didn't want to dwell on.

"I don't understand you, you know." Shannon was also watching Sammi walk away. "She's super hot. She's nice. She's clearly into you. And did I mention super hot? What's the problem?"

Keegan's brain tossed her an image then. A memory from nearly a year ago, the fumbling and the panic attack and the literal fucking disaster she and Sammi had agreed to never, ever mention again.

"You wouldn't understand," she said before she could think about how insulting that would sound. A flash of pain zipped across Shannon's face, and Keegan wanted to clarify by saying *You wouldn't understand because even I don't understand*, but she didn't. Instead, she grabbed Shannon's hand and said, "I think there are a couple of mini horses in the barn…"

It worked. Shannon's face lit up. "Why are we standing here then?"

Off to the barn they went.

❖

Why couldn't she forget about Keegan Duffy?

It was a thought that had floated around in Sammi's mind for the past eleven months, and she had no answer. Zip. Zero. Zilch. She didn't like to think about that night, how they'd gone on a date, finally, after running into each other such an inordinate number of times, there was no way *not* think the Universe was trying to tell them something. They'd had a fabulous dinner. The conversation had been riveting. She'd found Keegan to be funny and smart and as beautiful inside as she was outside. They'd gone back to Sammi's place for a nightcap. Honestly, Sammi hadn't planned that they'd end up making out on her couch—she just hadn't wanted the night with Keegan to end just yet.

But something had happened, and she still wasn't sure what it was. They'd been in full-on make-out mode, heavy kissing, wandering hands, clothing unbuttoned, and suddenly Keegan had stopped everything. Like, screeching halt. There were no other words for it. She'd pushed Sammi off her, slid herself away. She'd apologized, trying to verbalize…something. She'd used a lot of *I can't*s and *it's too much*es, and then she pleaded with Sammi that they never talk about it again. Ever. Weirdness, confusion, hurt. Sammi had felt all of it. And then Keegan had grabbed her jacket and left. Sammi had literally sat on the couch for the next fifteen minutes wondering what the hell had just happened and why.

She'd texted and Keegan hadn't ghosted her, so that was a plus, but Keegan hadn't really offered much of an explanation. And Sammi couldn't help but think that when somebody doesn't offer much of an explanation, it usually means the explanation is something they don't want to say out loud. That left Sammi feeling self-conscious and embarrassed. Had she pushed too hard? Had she turned Keegan off in some way? Oh God, *was she a terrible kisser?* That last one still fucked with her head, nearly a year later. Because how did you fix *that?*

After a couple weeks of sporadic texting, they'd eased into a sort of comfortable friendship. Sammi never brought up that night again—and neither did Keegan—but she'd be lying if she said it didn't sit in the back of her mind, pretty much twenty-four seven. She'd done her best to resign herself to never knowing what the hell had happened, and she'd packed that night up tightly in a box and put it on a high, high shelf in her memory bank. She accepted that she and Keegan were meant to be friends and nothing more, but that didn't mean she had to be okay with it.

And now Keegan was dating somebody named Jules.

Ugh.

"Jules." She sneered the name softly to herself. Ugh. Stupid Jules. What a stupid name.

"There you are." Her grandmother's voice came from some-where off to her right, and then Sammi saw her, making her way through the crowd, nodding and smiling and saying hello, because Mia Sorenson seemed to know half of Northwood, and she knew everybody involved with Junebug Farms.

"Hi, Grams." Sammi gave her a kiss on the cheek.

"You just get here?"

"About half an hour ago. I was just talking with Keegan and her sister, and then I was heading inside to check things out in there."

"Oh, Keegan's here?" Her grandmother pushed up onto her tiptoes—which didn't help much, given she was only five foot two—and scanned the crowd. Sammi suppressed an eye roll. Her grandma had always prided herself in her matchmaking skills—to be fair, she *had* matched up several happy couples—and she adored Keegan. She'd only met her a couple times, but she was constantly telling Sammi how good they'd be together. While Sammi had been too ashamed to tell her about that fateful night on the couch, she often had to steer the subject in another direction. Like now.

"Yeah, I think she's waiting for her girlfriend."

Her grandma's head snapped around, eyes wide. "She has a girlfriend?"

"She's dating somebody new now," Sammi said, forcing herself to sound nonchalant. "I told you that already, remember?"

"Oh. Well, that's not the same as having a girlfriend."

Sammi frowned. "It's not? How do you figure?"

"I mean, a girlfriend is a—hopefully—permanent resident. Dating somebody means you're still figuring things out. You know?"

"Hey, you two." Sammi's mother approached them from the opposite direction as her grandmother had. She was wearing a Junebug Farms sweatshirt with *Rescue a Heart* on it, along with line drawings of a dog, cat, horse, and guinea pig.

"Hi, Mom." She looked from one to the other. "You guys eat yet?"

Twenty minutes later, they were sitting at a picnic table eating bowls of poutine from the You're Poutine Me On truck.

"I feel like the food trucks are trying to top each other with the punny names." Sammi's mom forked a gravy-sodden fry into her mouth.

"They probably are."

"Oh!" Her grandma set her fork down and held out her hands, palms out, like she was stopping traffic. "I almost forgot to tell you…" She glanced around and lowered her voice a bit. "The shelter lost some state funding and is struggling to get more donations. I did tell you that. *But* they've got this fundraiser planned…" She explained everything to them, saying she'd learned it all from Jessica Barstow, the CEO. Then she looked at Sammi and said, "I may or may not have nominated you for queen."

"Oh my God, you didn't." Sammi closed her eyes. "Grandma."

"What? I happen to think you'd make a fantastic queen."

Her mother stood up. "I have to use the ladies' room, but before I go, I'd like to toss in my two cents. I also think you'd make a fabulous queen." And she flounced away laughing.

Sammi laughed, too. She couldn't help it. "I mean, I totally would, but who has the time?" She chewed a cheese curd.

"The cause is well worth it. You could make the time." Her

grandma turned away to scan the crowd. "Oh, there's Keegan." And before Sammi could stop her, she was waving and calling Keegan's name.

Since crawling under the picnic table to hide was probably unacceptable picnic etiquette, Sammi was forced to sit there and smile and try not to look uncomfortable. At least not as uncomfortable as Keegan looked as she approached their table.

"Well, hello there," she said cheerfully as she bent to give Sammi's grandma a kiss on the cheek.

"You here alone?" her grandma asked.

"No, my sister's with me." Keegan gestured absently off into the distance. "I think she found a high school friend she hasn't seen in a while."

"I heard you've been seeing somebody new."

Her grandma took a bite of her poutine, her gaze never leaving Keegan's, even as Sammi ground out, "Grandma!"

Keegan laughed softly, and her cheeks blossomed with pink circles. "Yeah. Guilty as charged."

Sammi's grandma made a show of looking around. "Where is she? Is she here with you?"

"Oh. Oh no." Keegan shook her head, and she seemed to be very carefully not looking at Sammi. "This isn't really...her thing."

"Saving abandoned animals isn't her thing?" her grandma said. "That's strange because it's very much yours, if I recall correctly from all your donations and your stint on the board and your field trips here with your students." She took another bite and kept her eyes on Keegan as she chewed. Sammi looked around for a hole she could crawl into. Maybe an alien spacecraft could beam her up right now. Please.

There was a beat of awkward before Keegan smiled and said, "Oh, there's my sister now. It was great seeing you again, Mrs. Sorenson." She gave Sammi a nod. "Sammi." And she headed across the lawn toward the main building. Sammi saw no sign of Keegan's sister, and once she was out of earshot, Sammi whipped around to her grandmother.

"Seriously?"

Her grandmother gave an innocent shrug. "What? I was just asking her some questions."

"Well, next time, just…don't. Okay?" Her appetite gone, she tossed the remainder of her poutine in the trash.

❖

Nope, not awkward at all.

Keegan shook her head as she walked. She had no idea where Shannon was—she just had to get out of there. Before she could dwell any longer on the mortification that had so clearly parked itself on Sammi's face, her phone pinged, then pinged again.

The first text was from Jules. *Hey, babe, what time are you done? Wanna do dinner?*

She'd been bummed that Jules hadn't wanted to accompany her to Junebug, even after she'd explained how much the place meant to her. She just wasn't really an animal person. That's what she'd said. *I'm just not really an animal person.* And she'd shrugged like she hadn't said something absolutely ludicrous. Some people didn't like animals. Right? That was fine. Totally allowed. Keegan could get past that. Sure she could.

The second text was from Sammi. *I'm so sorry*, was all it said, followed by a sad emoji.

Keegan had a quick flash of herself in the past saying exactly the same thing to Sammi. *I'm so sorry.* Ugh.

"There you are." Shannon's voice pulled her out of her head and back to the present.

"Hey. Hi. Where've you been?"

Shannon jerked a thumb over her shoulder toward the main building where she'd just come from. "Saw a friend from high school in there, so we were chatting. I also might have nominated you for the king and queen thing they're doing to fundraise." She gave a little giggle and headed to the left. "Come on. I wanna feed goats."

"You did not." Keegan hurried after her.

"Did," Shannon said when she'd caught up to her.

"Oh my God, why?"

"Because it might be fun." Shannon got herself a cup of feed for the goats. "But there were about a gazillion nominees, so don't worry. Your chances of winning are pretty slim. And why are you mad? You love this place."

"That's true," Keegan said with a sigh. She could feel Shannon's eyes on her.

"What's wrong?"

She shook her head. "Nothing. I think I'm just tired."

"You wanna bounce?"

"Soon. Jules wants to go to dinner."

It was Shannon's turn to shake her head. "I don't get why she's not here. She's just sitting at home on a weekend while the woman she's dating is out having fun and doing something she's passionate about. It's weird."

"It's not weird." Keegan watched a goat eat feed from Shannon's hand, daintily and adorably. "Okay, it's a little bit weird."

Shannon barked a laugh.

They spent a little while longer wandering the festival. So many people had their dogs with them, and seeing all the different breeds and mixes was incredibly interesting to Keegan. She wanted a dog. She had for a long time. An apartment wasn't ideal, though, so she'd hesitated and was still thinking about it. Plus, there were her two cats. She wasn't a hundred percent sure how they'd do with a dog. But she thought about it. One day…

Her phone pinged again, and she immediately felt bad she hadn't texted Sammi back. She pulled out her phone. Jules again. *Hello?*

Yeah, she hadn't texted her back either.

Shannon looked over her shoulder. "*Hello?* Wow. Rude much?"

"It's because I didn't answer her."

"So?"

Keegan ignored her sister as she typed, *Leaving soon. Dinner sounds good.*

Jules's text came back immediately. *Yay! Can't wait to see you,* and a heart emoji.

She looked up. "Ready to go?"

Shannon sighed loudly and made it clear she wasn't, but she went anyway, since Keegan was her ride. As they made their way to the car, Shannon waved to someone and Keegan followed her gaze. Sammi was near a vendor tent and waving good-bye to them.

The car doors shut, and Keegan pushed the ignition button.

"I like her," Shannon said.

"Who?"

"Sammi. She's so nice, and she's so hot, and I just don't understand why you don't hit that."

What Keegan didn't say was that she'd tried and then freaked out and ran out of Sammi's apartment in the literal middle of a make-out session. Shannon didn't know about that night. Nobody did. Not from her. God, it was so embarrassing, and the last thing she needed was to fall into a shame spiral from thinking about it.

No. Now there was Jules. She could be something, right? She was sweet. She was funny. She was attractive. But in order for her to be something, Keegan needed to step back from Sammi. She had a little bit recently, but only because of life. This might have to be more…intentional. It wasn't fair to Jules for her to have such a strong connection to somebody else. And she did. She did have a strong connection to Sammi. Too strong. And if she couldn't get past that night, what was the point? No, it was time to focus her attention on something—somebody—else.

She shifted the car into gear and headed to meet Jules for dinner.

Chapter Four

Oh my God, this looks amazing, Mom." Sammi wasn't kidding as she scooped a square of lasagna onto a plate and handed it across the table to her grandmother. "One order of veggie lasagna, ma'am."

Her grandma took it and set it in front of her while Sammi scooped out two more helpings. While her mother was not a vegetarian, nor was Sammi, they often ate meatless meals, especially when they ate with her grandma, who was a vegetarian.

"Your grandma told me what to do. I just followed orders," her mother said.

"First time for everything, right, Grams?"

Her grandma laughed.

It was a Monday evening in mid-November, and the weather had gone from crisp fall to brisk and chilly impending winter in a matter of weeks. Such was the change of seasons in the Northeast. *If you don't like the weather, wait five minutes. It'll change.* That was the motto in that neck of the woods, and it was true. And that made it a perfect night for lasagna.

They sat down to eat. Sammi didn't eat with them every night, but having her mother and grandmother living across the cul-de-sac had its perks. Mainly, she could have a home-cooked meal pretty much whenever she wanted if she was willing to simply cross the street.

"Hey, are we still on for the food truck rodeo at the Public Market this weekend?" her mother asked. "It is this weekend, right?"

"I texted Keegan to see if she wanted to join us, but I haven't heard back." The words had come out before she even realized they were ready to, and she could've kicked herself. She shoveled a big bite of lasagna into her mouth to keep from saying anything more.

"Didn't you invite her to your book club last week, too?" her grandmother asked.

Sigh. Of course her grandma wasn't going to let this go, which was why she should've kept her stupid mouth shut. "Yeah. She didn't answer that text either."

Her grandmother stared at her as she chewed for so long, it became almost creepy. Finally, she said simply, "I'm sorry, honey."

Sammi shrugged and did her best impression of nonchalant. "It's fine. She's got a girlfriend now, so I get why she doesn't want to do stuff with me." And she did. Kind of. It wasn't like they had ever been girlfriends. They were friends first. Had been for several years now. Did that mean they couldn't do anything together as friends because Keegan was seeing somebody?

Maybe it does. Maybe that's exactly what it means. Regardless, she could take a hint. She didn't need to be beaten over the head with twenty-seven unanswered texts. She was a smart woman. She got it.

"On a different note," her grandmother said, picking up her wineglass, "they'll be announcing the winners for the holiday king and queen next week at Junebug. Everybody's very excited. I get to help count votes."

"Oh, that'll be fun," Sammi said. "Don't rig the election so that you win."

"Listen, you, if I'd been nominated, I'd win by a landslide."

Sammi and her mother both laughed. "I don't doubt it, Grams. Not even a little bit." She topped off their wine. "What kinds of things will this royal couple have to do?"

Her grandma sat up a little straighter, and Sammi smiled. She'd hit on something her grandmother felt was important, sparked her passion. "All different holiday-themed things and visits. They'll have a dog or two from the shelter with them each time to raise awareness. Jessica asked some of us to make suggestions, and we came up with some terrific ideas. They'll make holiday cookies while partnered up with that dog bakery in Jefferson Square. They'll take presents to the sick kids in the pediatric wing of the hospital. They'll go sledding. They'll do a nursing home visit along with some carolers." At that last one, her grandma raised a hand and wiggled her fingers. "Yours truly included. And I think the last thing is riding on the float in the Christmas parade downtown."

"This is such a cute idea," her mom said. "And it's all to fundraise?"

Her grandma nodded, her eyes bright, her passion shining through even more. "With that loss of some state funding, they're struggling, and the shelter is practically full. Hopefully, this will help get them some money, as well as some notice."

"Maybe I'll end up adopting a dog after that," Sammi said with a grin. At her mother's surprised face, she said, "What? I've always wanted one. School made it hard. And then when I worked at the clinic, my hours were so crazy."

"And now, you're the boss," her grandma said with pride in her voice.

Sammi met her eyes. "And now, I'm the boss."

The conversation stayed on dogs and pets and Junebug Farms, and that was good because it kept Sammi from thinking about Keegan. She had to let that go. She knew she did. She'd always felt a strong connection to her, even after that catastrophic evening together, and if Keegan didn't want to date her, Sammi would settle for being friends. But now, it seemed like Keegan didn't even want that, and much as it stung, Sammi wasn't about to force her. She might be a big softie, but she had pride, and she wasn't going to beg for attention from Keegan. It made her sad, but what could she do?

Her mother and grandmother were talking about the lasagna now, so Sammi slipped her phone out of her pocket, and while she told herself she was checking her schedule for tomorrow, she also checked to see if Keegan had answered her last text. She hadn't.

With a sigh, she put her phone away and tuned herself back in to her family. She needed to put Keegan out of her mind—more importantly, out of her heart.

❖

"I am gonna eat so much food," Jules said as she and Keegan parked the car at the Public Market. "Look at all the trucks! I want something from all of them."

The childlike excitement in her eyes was cute, and it made Keegan smile. "How are we going to eat at every truck?"

"Sweetie, have you never been to a food truck rodeo before? They have samples. You can taste *everything*. It's brilliant." She grabbed Keegan's hand. "Come with me. I'm an old pro at this."

"How come?"

"My uncle had a food truck for years. He called it the Dog Park, 'cause he sold hot dogs while he was parked. Get it?"

"I do."

"I used to help him out on weekends. It can be a brutal job. The truck gets hot inside. There's not a lot of room to work. But I loved it. We used to do rodeos all the time. They're a good way to drum up business." They weaved their way through what looked like it could end up being a sizable crowd, despite the cold temperatures. Jules stopped when they reached the start of a long row lined with food trucks. "Where would you like to begin?"

"You're the pro," Keegan said. "You lead the way. I'll follow."

"Awesome. We'll start with something to keep us warm."

Soon, they had hot chocolate in their hands, and they'd slowed their pace to a stroll. Jules was reading the menu on the side of the Cluck Truck, which specialized in, unsurprisingly, fried chicken. Keegan held the hot chocolate in both hands, letting it warm her palms, as she watched her date.

Jules was attractive. Dark blond hair cut short in the back and a little longer on top. It flopped into her eyes often, and she had the habit of tossing her head sideways to clear her vision. She was taller than Keegan, tall and lean, built like a runner, though she said she hated running, and if there was ever a zombie apocalypse, she'd be one of the first to die because everybody would run faster than her. Her eyes were big and blue, set close together, and her mouth was small, her lips thin. Today, she wore jeans, a blue winter jacket, and a Buffalo Bills knit hat with a red pom-pom on the top. She was very cute, and when she turned and met Keegan's gaze with bright eyes, a big smile, and that childlike excitement she'd had ever since they'd decided to come, Keegan felt...nothing.

Before she could even think about what that might mean, a voice cut through the air.

"Apparently, they'll let anybody in here, huh?"

Keegan turned and met the kind eyes of Mia Sorenson, fellow Junebug Farms volunteer. And Sammi's grandmother. She was all bundled up in a big, black puffy coat and a white hat. "Hi, Mia," she said with a grin, then indicated her with a hand. "Clearly, yes, they're letting in all the riffraff today."

Mia laughed, her breath vaporizing in the air, and gave her a playful shove as a younger woman caught up to her and, holy good God, she looked like Sammi in thirty years. "I don't know if you've ever met my daughter. Keegan, this is Maggie. Maggie, this is Keegan Duffy."

"Oh, *this* is Keegan," Maggie said cryptically and held out her hand to shake. "It's nice to meet you."

"Same," Keegan said to the woman with familiar dark eyes. She looked past her as she asked, "Is Sammi here with you?"

Maggie nodded. "She's around here somewhere."

Mia pointed vaguely. "I saw her and Chrissy over by that sushi truck a few minutes ago."

Her and Chrissy. Keegan tried to remember Sammi mentioning a Chrissy, but came up empty. "Oh. Well, maybe I'll see her." The clearing of a throat behind her snagged her attention, and she turned to meet Jules's expectant gaze. "Oh. Right. Sorry. Jules, this is Mia and Maggie. Mia and I met at Junebug Farms."

"Hi. Jules. I'm Keegan's girlfriend," Jules said.

"Date. She's my date." She felt more than saw Jules's head snap around to her, and she knew they'd be having a discussion later. So did Mia, apparently, by the amused expression on her face.

"Um, how's the hot chocolate?" Mia asked, clearly trying to change the subject, and Keegan wanted to hug her for it.

"God, it's delicious. So rich. And warm, which is key in this weather."

"We were thinking of getting some, so that's a good endorsement. What foods have you sampled?"

"None yet." She turned to make sure Jules was included in the conversation. "But Jules here is a pro, so I'm letting her lead the way, and I think"—she indicated behind them—"we're gonna start with some chicken." She turned to Jules. "Yeah?"

Jules nodded and smiled, but stayed quiet, and Keegan knew she'd hurt her feelings.

"Well, we'll leave you to it while we go find the hot chocolate." Mia squeezed Keegan's forearm as she met Jules's gaze. "Lovely to meet you, Jules."

"Same."

Keegan watched as Mia and Maggie wandered away, and she wondered where Sammi was. The idea that she was here was messing with her head, so she forced herself to focus on Jules. "So. Chicken?" She indicated the nearby sample table containing little plastic plates with bites of fried chicken on them.

"Sure."

They each grabbed a plate and ate, Jules much less exuberant than she'd been just ten minutes before.

All right, time to deal.

"Are you upset with me?" she asked quietly.

Jules sighed. "I'm not upset. Just a little stung."

"Fair. But don't you think we should have a discussion before referring to each other as girlfriends?" Jules's eyes went wide, so it was clear she disagreed, and that got under Keegan's skin. "We've only been on a few dates, Jules."

Jules's shoulders dropped in defeat, and she gazed down at her boots. "I know. I just...I really like you, you know?"

"I like you, too."

"I didn't think using that word was a big deal." She punctuated that with a shrug.

"It's a bit fast for me."

"Okay. Good to know."

Keegan watched as Jules's face went from gently hurt to slightly angry. Okay, that was interesting. Keegan didn't agree with Jules when she was gentle, so Jules went hard instead. Something Keegan should file away, definitely.

"Next truck?" Hard and cold, as Jules started walking, leaving Keegan behind with her chicken.

"Yeah, this is gonna be a fun day," she muttered as she tossed her garbage into a nearby can and followed Jules.

❖

"Do you think they offer rooms in this food truck?" Chrissy asked as she took a bite of her pulled mock-pork slider and looked longingly at the menu. "'Cause I could live here. In this truck. And eat these every day." She popped the rest into her mouth, then looked longingly at the girl holding the tray of samples. The girl laughed and rolled her eyes and gave Chrissy another slider. Chrissy squealed in delight and took a bite. "I had no idea you could make jackfruit taste like pulled pork. How is that possible? Also, what the fuck is jackfruit?"

Sammi laughed at her friend, whom she'd known since their early days of clinic work. "I don't have an answer to either question. But my grandma's a vegetarian, and she'd love this." Sammi stood on her toes, trying to look over the tops of heads to see if she could find her grandma and mother who were around here somewhere.

"Hey," came her mother's voice from behind her.

"Oh, hey." Sammi turned to meet them. "Grams, you've gotta try these."

They got more slider samples, and there was a chorus of *mmm*s and *yum*s for the next few minutes as they ate.

She smiled as she watched her grandmother enter into a conversation with the sample-holding girl about jackfruit, what it was, and where she could find it. Chrissy was on her fourth sample slider when Sammi's mom said, "We saw Keegan a bit ago."

Traitor that it was, Sammi's heart skipped a beat, even as she worked hard to keep her expression neutral. "Oh yeah?"

Her mother nodded. "She was with Jules, who seems…" She shrugged.

"Who seems what? Nice? Awful? Like her soulmate? Evil? What?"

Chrissy leaned in and feigned a stage whisper as she said to Sammi's mom, "Your daughter is clearly not invested in this at all."

Sammi frowned. She'd promised herself to let the whole Keegan thing go, and at the mere mention of her name, that promise had flown right out the window.

"She seems difficult," her mom finally settled on.

"Oh." Not the descriptor Sammi was expecting.

"That was delicious," her grandmother said, rejoining the conversation. "I'm going to try to make these next week." She glanced at her daughter-in-law. "Onward?"

"Yes, ma'am," Sammi's mother replied, and they started walking, Sammi and Chrissy following a bit behind.

"Keegan's the one you had that fling with last year, yeah?" Chrissy asked.

"It was barely a fling. It was dinner and an evening that ended in…I don't even know what." She touched Chrissy's arm until she met her gaze. She lowered her voice to a whisper and asked, "Do you think I'm just, like, a terrible kisser or something?"

"Oh, sweetie, no. I'm sure that's not it. Sounds to me like she had some of her own issues she was dealing with." Chrissy took a beat before adding, "I'm kind of surprised you're still hung up on this."

"I know. It's just…we've stayed friends. We have lunch or dinner here and there, and we text a bit." She gave a soft snort. "Or we did until she started seeing this Jules. Now she doesn't answer my texts at all."

"Babe, I hate to say it, but I think you need to let this go. Sounds like she's giving you hints you're not taking. You deserve somebody present, you know?"

Sammi inhaled a deep breath and let it out slowly. "I know. You're right." Chrissy *was* right. She wasn't sure why she continued to cling to the idea of somebody who clearly didn't want anything to do with her. Yes, she'd thought their connection—which was genuine and strong, and she was sure Keegan felt that, too—meant something more than it did, but evidently she'd been wrong. "I guess I just needed to hear it from somebody on the outside. You're right." Shifting her attitude entirely, she sniffed the air. "Do you smell that?"

Chrissy started sniffing, too. "I do! Oh my God, is that…is it… the doughnut truck?"

"I believe it is, my friend. I believe it is."

"We must find it!"

"We must!" They were so loud and dramatic that the people around them started looking and smiling. And if anything could take Sammi's mind off negative things, it was a freshly made doughnut.

CHAPTER FIVE

It was the Wednesday before Thanksgiving, so the overall atmosphere at Junebug Farms was festive and celebratory. Nobody was really doing much actual work. Most people were chatting and visiting and eating some of the many snacks people brought in.

Mia knew this would be the case until after New Year's, when she used to be the kind of person who realized with horror just how many Christmas cookies she'd eaten over the past month and then would become a fiend at the gym. No more of that nonsense. No. The holidays were meant for enjoyment and celebration, and the size of her hips was so unimportant in the grand scheme of life. She wished she'd learned that so much sooner than she had.

She and Beth had been walking a couple of very sweet shelter dogs, both pit bull mixes. Lisa didn't like them to be called that because, in actuality, that was an umbrella term for several bully breeds—American Staffordshire terrier, American pit bull terrier, and Staffordshire bull terrier, to name a few. They got such a bad rap, but Lisa had explained that if they were raised right, they were loving and affectionate dogs. Mia didn't always love walking them, but only because they were such strong animals, and she was merely one tiny woman. But today's was a gentle giant named Hulk, slate gray with soulful eyes and goofy ears. He was an old guy, a senior dog, and he seemed to get that she was a bit nervous, so he took his time, continually glancing back at Mia to check if he was doing okay.

She was in love in a heartbeat.

Back inside, she was about to unleash Hulk when she heard the clicking of heels on the cement floor of the dog wing and looked up to see Jessica headed her way.

"Good afternoon, ladies," she said. "Can I ask a favor of you both?"

"Of course," Mia told her, rubbing Hulk's velvety ears between her fingers. Then she kissed his head and closed the door to his kennel, feeling a little pang in her chest.

Beth closed the kennel to her dog, too. "Whatever you need."

"Great." Jessica seemed slightly out of breath, though she always seemed like that to Mia, the poor girl. She ran herself ragged taking care of this place. She loved it with everything she had. Anybody could see that. But some days, it seemed like it was an awful lot. "We're tallying up the votes for the Junebug Farms holiday king and queen. I've got all the computer votes counted, but there were some last minute old-school paper votes that came either in the mail or were left by visitors and other people who couldn't make Barktoberfest. They're in a box in my office. I've left the computer tally open on my monitor, but I have an off-site meeting in"—she checked her watch and blanched—"gah, ten minutes ago. Would you two mind just finishing the count? I shouldn't be long, but I'd like to get this done so I can call the winners on Friday and make sure they're up for the tasks ahead."

"I have time," Beth said, then looked to Mia. "You?"

Mia waved a dismissive hand. "Consider it done."

"You guys are the best. I don't know what I'd do without you. Thank you so much." She gave them each a hug and hurried back the way she'd come.

"I worry about her," Beth said. "She takes on too much."

Mia nodded. "I think this cut to the state funding has caused her a lot of stress." They started down the hall toward the exit, cooing to various dogs as they went, stopping to pet a couple through the fence doors of the kennels. "I do like the idea of this fundraiser awareness thing for the holidays, though. Could really help."

"Man, I hope so. I don't know what happens if there isn't

enough money. Does the shelter shut down? They wouldn't do that, would they?"

The thought took the little seed of worry she already had and multiplied it. "I have no idea. I hope not." She wouldn't just be sad for all the animals who would lose their spaces, would probably be shipped off to other shelters that were maybe not no-kill—she'd be sad for herself. She spent so much time at Junebug. It was a part of her. The thought of losing it was unbearable. "Hopefully, this holiday campaign will work and bring in a bunch of money."

"Maybe the king and queen will be very rich people and will hand over a fortune."

"God, wouldn't that be nice." Mia held the door of Jessica's office open for Beth, and they went inside.

As promised, Jessica's computer was up and there were two lists on her monitor, one of potential queens and one of potential kings, along with the number of votes each had so far. There was also a stack of mail and a small box containing several folded scraps of paper. Mia sat down behind Jessica's big desk as Beth came around and stood behind her.

"Hey, look, your granddaughter is in second place for queen," Beth said, pointing at the screen.

Sure enough, there was Sammi's name, right behind the owner of a local restaurant Mia was familiar with. "Well, would you look at that."

"I'm not surprised. Everybody loves Dr. Sammi." Beth squeezed Mia's shoulder. "Okay, how do you want to do this?" Beth asked.

"Why don't you give me the box? I'll count those votes and you do the mail."

"Deal." Beth went around to the front of the desk and took a seat there, then handed the box of slips to Mia. As she looked over the names on the list again, she noticed the name right behind Sammi's.

Keegan Duffy.

She was only a few votes behind Sammi. And when Mia looked

at the list for kings, Keegan also had more votes than the top guy on that list.

Interesting. And just like that, a tiny kernel of an idea began to take shape.

It took about half an hour to go through all the slips and all the mail, tally them up, and when they did, Mia sat there and blinked at the computer monitor.

Sammi had won queen, and she told Beth as much.

"Oh my God, Mia, that's amazing! How fun!" Beth clapped her hands together and did a little shimmy in her chair. Then she asked about the king.

Before she could stop herself, Mia typed a couple of quick keystrokes, which moved Keegan's name to the opposite column, and said, "Keegan Duffy. Oh, hang on…"

Beth furrowed her brow. "Wait. Keegan's a woman." She got up and came around the desk to look over Mia's shoulder.

Mia blew out a breath as she nodded. "She is. But look." She pointed at the final numbers of all the votes tallied up. "Keegan has more votes than the highest man, and she's just under Sammi."

"She has *way* more votes than any of the men—they both do," Beth confirmed, rubbing her chin with her fingertips. "She must've been put in the wrong category by somebody. Her name is gender-neutral, so it makes sense that could happen. What do you think we should do?"

If she gave voice to her idea, there'd be no turning back. Mia knew this. She couldn't suggest what she was about to suggest and then shrug and let it go if she was met with resistance. No, she'd have to stand firm and battle if necessary, though she didn't think she'd need to do that with Jessica, for obvious reasons. She took a deep breath, turned to Beth, and said, "I think we leave it as is. I think we tell Jessica these are the final results—because they are."

"And we have two queens."

"And we have two queens."

Beth took a moment and seemed to roll it around for a bit before nodding with a grin. "I like it. And who knows? Maybe it'll bring a bit more attention to Junebug for being progressive."

"Oh, I like that." The part she left unsaid: *If anybody* does *have an issue, they're not going to want to come across as even the tiniest bit homophobic to the lesbian CEO of Junebug Farms, so they will likely keep their mouths shut.* And the best part of all, which she also left unsaid, was that Sammi and Keegan would now be spending a lot of time together doing holiday things with dogs. Because that's all they needed, Mia was sure. Just a little more time together.

It was already crystal clear to her that Jules was *not* it for Keegan. She just needed a little help to see that maybe Sammi was. She took great pride in her matchmaking skills. Somehow, she could see when two people should be together. To date, she'd matched up six different couples. They were all still together. A one hundred percent success rate. Okay, she had to finagle things a bit here. It wasn't like Keegan didn't get more votes, so Mia wasn't taking the king spot away from anybody. It was just a teeny tiny edit. That's all.

And if it worked the way she thought it would, it was totally worth it.

She sat back in Jessica's chair and surveyed her handiwork, the lists with Sammi's and Keegan's names at the tops.

With a nod, she looked at Beth and smiled. "It's done."

CHAPTER SIX

K eegan loved the Friday after Thanksgiving. She'd loved it as a kid, and she loved it now, as an adult who worked in the school system. It was like a vacation day from her vacation day.

Thanksgiving was always spent with her family. Her mother, father, Shannon, her mother's mother, and her father's sister. They always spent the day together, watching football and playing cards and having a huge, traditional Thanksgiving dinner with all the trimmings. They used to alternate houses, but with her grandmother getting older and Keegan living in an apartment that was perfect for her but not so perfect for entertaining more than a couple people at a time, they'd ended up at her parents' house the past three years in a row. She didn't think her mom minded, given how much she enjoyed cooking for people. Thanksgiving Day was for family, where she came from.

The Friday after, however? Yeah, that day was just for her. She had a group of teacher friends who always tried every year to get her to go Black Friday shopping—and no, there weren't enough sales in the world to get her to do that—so she declined every year. Shannon always tried to get her to come over again, to hang with her because she didn't want to get roped into helping their mom make turkey soup. Needless to say, Shannon did *not* enjoy cooking for other people. And Keegan always managed to dodge that plea and stay home.

She hummed happily as she dragged her Rubbermaid totes full of Christmas decorations out of the closet in her spare bedroom.

There were also a few boxes in her storage space in the basement—she'd get them later. Right now, she had her cup of coffee, some soft jazz playing, Cocoa and Bean, her cats, lounging on the back of the couch in a sunbeam, facing each other like mirror sphinxes, and she was happy. She had today plus a weekend before she had to go back to work, and she had nowhere to be today. Absolute bliss.

She had just shifted some plants a bit to make room for her Christmas tree in front of the window when her phone rang. She chuckled as she pulled the bottom piece of her tree out of its box. "You hear that, boys?" she said to her cats. "That's Aunt Shannon with her annual *Please help me, I can't be alone with Mom all day* phone call." But when she grabbed her cell, it wasn't Shannon's face on the screen. The number was labeled *Junebug Farms*.

"Hello?" she answered, wondering if this was a call for donations.

"Hi there, can I speak to Keegan Duffy please?" The voice was female, warm and friendly, and vaguely familiar.

"Speaking."

"Hi, Ms. Duffy, this is Jessica Barstow from Junebug Farms?"

Aha! "Oh, hey, Ms. Barstow. How was your Thanksgiving?"

"Jessica, please. It was very nice, thank you. And yours?"

"Same. And please call me Keegan. Ms. Duffy is what my students call me." They both chuckled politely, and Keegan asked, "What can I do for you, Jessica?" Because while she'd been solicited by phone in the past by Junebug, her call had never come from the CEO herself. She was super curious.

"Well, I don't know if you're aware, but we're having a holiday fundraising campaign here at Junebug, including electing a holiday king and queen to do some holiday things in public with some of our adoptable dogs. We're hoping to make the shelter more visible, do some social media posting, hopefully get some interviews on the local news and with the local papers, that kind of thing, to help raise awareness and, of course, money."

"I do remember hearing about that." Keegan donated to the shelter every year, sometimes a couple times a year, and she always petitioned to take her students on field trips there. "Are you asking for a donation? I just donated a couple months ago, but I might be able to spare—"

"Oh no! God, no. I would never ask you to give money when you already have. No, I'm calling to tell you that you're one half of Junebug's royal couple."

"Me?" Keegan couldn't believe it. "Are you sure?"

Jessica laughed, a sound that was gentle and kind. "I'm positive. You came in just behind the other half of the couple. We counted twice. Promise. So, this call is to see if you're interested. It's gonna take a bit of your free time, I'm afraid, but it would help us so, so much. You've been such a friend to the shelter, donating your money and your time and bringing your students. You're somebody we trust with this task. And if you *are* interested, and you have some time—say, tomorrow?—to come by the shelter, we can talk about what we have scheduled, see what works and what doesn't, that kind of thing."

"Are you kidding me? I love this! I think it's a fantastic idea, and I'm so excited I get to be a part of it. Thank you so much!"

It was the truth. She considered herself a fairly generous person. She wasn't rich by any stretch, but if she had money to spare and could help somebody, she would. Her mother had taught her early on what it meant to help the less fortunate, and young Keegan had been surprised by how good it made her feel to help somebody else. She and Jessica set up a time the next morning to go over all the details, and by the time she hung up, she was grinning like the proverbial fool.

Doing fun holiday activities with dogs? Yes, please. Sign her up!

❖

Jessica Barstow was very pretty.

Sammi had always thought so. She was tall, her hair a rich shade of auburn. She'd be called a redhead by most, but it was more a deep copper, a soft rust color that not a lot of people had. She was maybe in her midforties, and her blue eyes seemed like they held many stories. Sammi could only imagine the things she'd seen, running an animal shelter, not all of them pleasant.

She'd harbored a tiny crush on Jessica for a while when she'd first started coming to Junebug Farms. Nothing outrageous, just a genuine admiration for a very attractive woman who'd made quite a name for herself locally. And when Sammi had met Jessica's wife, Sydney, she understood in an instant how perfect they were together, and she went from crushing on Jessica to hoping, one day, she'd have something like what they had.

It was the Saturday after Thanksgiving at not quite ten in the morning when she pulled into the Junebug Farms parking lot. It wasn't buzzing yet, but it would be. It always was on Saturdays, people coming to look at the animals up for adoption, trying to make that difficult decision of which one. As she got out of her car, she saw a car roll past the building and around the back, following a sign marked *Animal Surrender*. Sammi took in a deep breath of cold November air, filling her lungs before she let it out slowly and tried to give whoever was in that car the benefit of the doubt if they were about to leave their pet here for good.

The idea of some poor dog or cat being abandoned here by their person squeezed her heart a bit, and she did her best to shake it off as she headed for the main entrance, shifting her focus back to the fact that she had won holiday queen, pretty freaking cool and totally unexpected, and she couldn't quite keep the smile from her face as she walked in.

"Good morning," she said to the woman at the front desk. "I have an appointment with Jessica Barstow. Samantha Sorenson."

"Ah yes, Dr. Sorenson, good to see you. Jessica will meet you in the conference room." She pointed to a hallway off the main lobby. "Just down there. First door on the right."

"Got it. Thanks." Sammi headed in the direction the woman had pointed and found the door marked *Conference Room* without issue. It was slightly ajar, and when she pushed it open, she stopped in her tracks, surprised. "Hi?" she said, not meaning it to be a question, but that's how it came out.

Keegan smiled at her from her seat at the big conference table.

"Sammi? Hi." The confusion and surprise on her face must have rivaled Sammi's. "What are—"

Before she could finish her sentence, Sammi felt a hand on her back and there was Jessica Barstow, looking as confident and no-nonsense as always, and she gently nudged Sammi into the room. "Good morning, friends," she said, her voice cheerful. "It's so good to see you both. Thanks for giving up some of your Saturday to come see me." She walked all the way in and grabbed a chair, then indicated another one and said to Sammi, "Have a seat." She gestured with her chin to a table against the wall that held a Keurig and all the ingredients for hot beverages. "Please help yourself to coffee, tea, hot cocoa, whatever." She had a folder in front of her, and she folded her hands over it as she met first Sammi's gaze and then Keegan's.

"So. I bet you're each wondering what the other is doing here."

Sammi exchanged a glance with Keegan, then they both nodded.

"Here's the deal. You were both nominated in our contest. Only you, Keegan, your votes were accidentally tallied into the race for *king*. Somebody who isn't familiar with you must've assumed you were a man and dropped you into that category."

Keegan's smile was soft and she nodded. "Wouldn't be the first time." She began to push to her feet.

"Wait. Where are you going?"

Keegan stopped, mid-rise. "Oh. I just figured you wanted to tell me the mix-up face to face. I assume Sammi won the race for queen."

Jessica gestured for her to sit back down. "She did." She turned to Sammi. "Congratulations."

"Thanks." Sammi grinned but was still confused.

"You, however," Jessica said, returning her gaze to Keegan, "won the race for king. You beat all the men by a significant margin and came in a mere two votes behind Sammi."

"My mom and grandma," Sammi said, and Jessica laughed.

"Probably true. Anyway, I sat down with my board. While it would've been easy to just announce the winner of the king race, we didn't think it was fair to have the king be somebody who received far fewer votes than Keegan. And also—selfishly—I thought it might be kind of cool and progressive of us to have two queens this year." She arched a precisely shaped eyebrow and added, "It's not like they were going to argue against that with *me*, who has a wife. They agreed. Happily, I'm proud to say." She tapped the closed folder in front of her. "Now, if either of you is uncomfortable with this arrangement, just say so. There will be no hard feelings, and we can move on to the person with the next most votes."

Sammi couldn't believe this. At all. How? How had this happened? Was the Universe smiling on her? Was it fucking with her? Because it could be either right now, and she wasn't sure which. All she did know was that, as long as Keegan didn't stand up and leave right now, Sammi was going to be spending more time with her for the next few weeks. And that absolutely did not suck. She inhaled quietly and turned to meet Keegan's blue eyes.

"I'm totally good with it," Keegan said. "You?"

"I'm in," Sammi said, trying not to smile as hugely as she wanted to.

"Fantastic," Jessica said with a slap on the folder. "Perfect. Thank you both so much. Okay, here's the itinerary for the coming weeks." She passed them each a sheet of paper. "I know paper is old school, but I like to be able to hold something in my hand when I'm talking. Don't worry, I'll also text it to each of you once we finish this meeting. I'd like you to check all the dates. I know we're getting into the Christmas season and people get busy and have parties and things to go to, so let me know as early on as you can if you're unable to make something on the list. We'll figure out an alternative. You'll see some things are scheduled on the weekends and some are on weeknights. I know you both have day jobs, so we didn't schedule anything during your lunch hours or whatever." She gave a chuckle, and it was in that moment—something about the tone or the sound of it—that Sammi realized Jessica was nervous and stressed, and she wondered if the shelter was in worse shape than her grandmother had said. "We've got some fun stuff lined up, and at each event, you'll have a dog or two from the shelter that's available for adoption. Somebody from our marketing firm will accompany you on most outings so they can take photos and video, upload to social media, stuff like that. The name of the game here is publicity, but we didn't want to put that pressure on you. You're not responsible for any of it. So you just attend the events with the dogs, smile, make small talk, whatever. The marketing folks will take care of the rest." She finally stopped and took a deep breath. "We need to raise money. As much as we can."

Sammi wanted nothing more than to scrub that expression of worry off Jessica's face. "Well, I think it's gonna be great. I can't wait. How about you?" She turned to Keegan, whose grin was big.

"Absolutely. I'm excited. This'll be fun. And hopefully, we'll raise a fortune."

The relief on Jessica's face was as clear as if the word *relieved* had been written on her forehead in red marker. "Oh, thank you both so much." She stood up and shook their hands. "You have no idea what this means to the shelter. Seriously. Thank you."

Twenty minutes later, Sammi and Keegan were headed back out to their cars, deep green Junebug Farms fleece jackets in hand— thank you gifts from Jessica that she also asked they wear on their excursions.

"Well, that was unexpected," Keegan said.

"Right?" Sammi agreed. "I did not see that coming."

They reached Sammi's car first, and Keegan stopped with her. "Are you sure you're okay with this?" she asked, putting a hand on Sammi's arm.

Sammi gave a little snort. "Of course. Why wouldn't I be?" Keegan held her gaze, seemed to be looking for something in her eyes. "Seriously. It's gonna be fun. Don't you think? Wait. Are *you* okay with this? What will Jules think?" Gah! Yeah, that last question was supposed to be an inside thought, but it had slipped out.

Keegan's blue eyes didn't go hard, but they definitely lost a bit of sparkle. "Jules isn't the boss of me." She glanced down at her feet, and a soft smile came to her lips. "As my students would say."

Sammi laughed. "Fair enough." She glanced down at the sheet Jessica had given them. "Looks like our first event is Tuesday night.

We're going to the mall to help with gift wrapping." She groaned. "I suck at wrapping."

"I do not suck at wrapping," Keegan said in a little singsong voice.

"Figures."

There was a moment of silence, and they just held one another's gaze until Keegan finally said, "Well. I guess I'll see you Tuesday, then."

"I guess you will." Sammi watched Keegan walk to her car, and she waited until she was safely inside and had started the engine before she got into her own car. With a glance at herself in the rearview mirror, she shook her head. "*I guess you will?* God. You are *so* not smooth."

❖

"I thought the rice was a little dry, didn't you?" Mia said loudly from the kitchen as she poured two glasses of cabernet. She carried them out to the living room and handed one to Maggie. "I think I overcooked it by a few minutes." When Maggie didn't comment, just continued to stare out the window at the street, Mia noticed that her daughter-in-law had that little divot between her eyebrows that said she was worried about something. Mia had noticed it almost the first week she'd met Maggie, when Kevin had brought her home to meet his parents. She'd been trying to remember the name of a book she'd wanted to recommend to Mia, probably wanting to impress her, and that little dent had appeared, just above the bridge of her nose. "What?"

"I'm worried about her." It was easy to ascertain who Maggie was referring to, as she was gazing across the cul-de-sac at Sammi's house. Then she turned and met Mia's gaze. "You didn't have anything to do with the results of the voting, did you?" She narrowed her eyes just enough to let Mia know she was suspicious.

Mia took a sip of her wine before answering, "Of course not." And she made sure to look indignant. "All Beth and I did was keep the results as they were. Keegan had been put in the men's category when we did the tally." Okay, maybe that wasn't quite the whole truth. She didn't tell Maggie that Keegan had ended up in the men's category because she'd put her there. "Honestly, I think it'll be good for the shelter. Being progressive, especially these days, should bring in some younger donors. And Keegan did win more votes than any of the men. By a lot. It was the only fair result." And after Beth had left, it hadn't taken much more than a nudge to convince Jessica to leave the results as they were and take them to the board. Which she'd done. And now, Sammi and Keegan were going to spend a ton of time together…

"I just don't want her hurt." Maggie's voice interrupted Mia's self-congratulatory flashbacks. "Again." Maggie's gaze met hers. "You know how she feels about Keegan, and it's been pretty clear Keegan doesn't feel the same way."

Oh, I don't know about that. She almost said it out loud, but that would clue Maggie in that maybe her mother-in-law wasn't quite as innocent as she was making herself out to be. But again, Mia prided herself—if only privately—on her ability to recognize a perfect match when she saw one. And if it needed a little help, some slight intervention, in order to make it happen, she was all too happy to provide it.

Her work here was done. Now, all she had to do was sit back and watch it all unfold. She sipped her wine to hide her smile.

❖

Keegan was nervous.

Why? Why was she nervous? What was there to be nervous about? She shoved her gearshift into park and sat there, letting the car idle in the early December evening. The heater was up high and set for the floor, because she'd worn boots for the way they looked rather than their ability to keep her feet warm. She hadn't even begun the evening yet, and her feet were already freezing. She hoped that wasn't an omen.

Sammi's car was already in the Junebug parking lot. She'd recognized it as she'd pulled in. A glance at her phone told her it was six thirty-four. She was supposed to meet Sammi and the marketing people here, gather their dogs, and they'd all ride together to the mall in one of the Junebug Farms vans. She flipped her visor down and took a moment to check her hair in the mirror. She'd gone with a look she called classy casual: jeans, ankle boots, and an emerald green top that she'd been told accented her auburn hair perfectly. Her Junebug Farms fleece jacket was actually cuter and more stylish than she'd expected, and it went well with her top. She pulled out a tube of her favorite lip gloss and swiped it over her bottom lip, refusing to entertain the question her brain was asking her—*for who? the dogs?*—and then fluffed her hair and smoothed each eyebrow with a fingertip. She pulled out her phone and saw no messages from Jules. With a sigh, she put it away, turned off the car, and headed inside.

Most of Keegan's visits to Junebug Farms happened either on the weekend or when she brought a class for a field trip, during a school day. She couldn't recall ever having been there in the evening during the week, and it was noticeably quieter than she was used to it being. Still noisy, though. There was still endless barking, but not nearly as many people wandering around or phones ringing off the hook. Her eyes immediately fell on Sammi, standing at the horseshoe-shaped front desk with a couple other people and laughing at something the woman behind it had said. Sammi wore her Junebug jacket, too, which looked great on her, and she turned then and met Keegan's gaze, and something inside Keegan fluttered with recognition.

"There she is," Sammi said, clearly happy to see her. Keegan tried to recall the last time somebody had been so obviously glad about her presence. "I knew you wouldn't stand me up."

"Never," she said, catching Sammi's megawatt smile. The two people next to her were likely the marketing folks, as the man had his iPhone out and was already taking shots of the lobby, the sign behind the desk, Sammi. The woman also had her phone out, and she was typing even as she sporadically glanced up to show that she was paying attention.

"So," Sammi said, "since I was here first and you were late"— she winked at Keegan—"and Lisa is getting our dogs, I will make the introductions. Keegan Duffy, this is Evan Anderson." She indicated the guy taking photos. "He's our photographer for these excursions."

Evan was maybe in his late twenties. His sandy hair was a bit on the shaggy side, almost surfer-like, and his nose looked like it had been broken at least once. His smile was friendly, and his front teeth had a slight overlap, which honestly only made his face more interesting. Shannon would be falling all over herself right now to talk to him. The thought made Keegan smile as she reached out and shook his hand. "Nice to meet you, Evan."

"Likewise," he said.

"And this is Grace Curtis," Sammi said, gesturing to the woman.

Grace had dark hair, and when she smiled at Keegan, deep dimples appeared. "So nice to meet you, Keegan," she said as they shook hands. "I hope you're looking forward to this. It's gonna be fun."

Keegan's nerves had settled down to a dull hum that buzzed through her body as the door to the dog wing opened and Lisa came into the lobby, two leashes in hand, a dog at the end of each, one big and one small. The big dog was walking calmly at Lisa's side. The little one had left zero slack in the leash and apparently had places to be, if his straining legs had anything to say about it.

"Hi there," Lisa said, looking friendly and exhausted, and this was the way she'd appeared any time Keegan had seen her. With her was a man who looked to be in his early to mid-twenties. His dark hair was pulled back into a man bun and he sported a neatly trimmed beard and black-rimmed glasses. "Here are your charges for the evening," Lisa said as she held up the leash holding the large dog. "This is Beckett. People are going to ask you if he's a pit bull because he clearly looks like one. You tell them *pit bull* is an umbrella term, and Beckett is a Staffordshire terrier or Staffy. Got it?" When they all nodded, she indicated the other dog. "This is Binky, and as you can see, walks are her favorite thing in life. We think she's part Chihuahua and part…something else. And she's super loving." She held up her phone. "I've texted you both all the

details we have on these two, in case people ask, and this is Trent."
She gestured to Mr. Man Bun. "He's going to be driving you guys
to all your events and he'll have the details on all the animals you
take, so if you have questions—or if a potential adopter or donor has
questions you can't answer—refer them to Trent. Okay?"

Trent smiled and shook the hands of all four of them. He had
a slight twitch that made him blink a lot, Keegan noticed, but his
expression was friendly and his eyes were kind. "It's great to meet
you all. Are we ready to go?" At their enthusiastic nods, he said,
"Great. I'll pull the van up out front. Meet you in five." And he
disappeared back through the door that led to the dog wing.

"I'm excited," Sammi said, lifting her shoulders and giving
her a huge grin, like a little kid headed for a shopping spree in a
toy store. It was damn cute, and Keegan couldn't help but smile,
Sammi's happy energy contagious.

"Me too," she said, and it was true.

Ten minutes later, they were all loaded into the Junebug Farms
van, dogs in crates in the back—not something Binky was happy
about, if her annoyed barks were any indication—and people seat
belted into their seats. Keegan and Sammi sat close in the middle
section, and Sammi's thigh was warm against Keegan's. She tried
not to notice that but failed miserably.

"So," Trent said from the driver's seat as he drove. He met
Keegan's eyes briefly in the rearview mirror. "A little background
on each dog, yeah?" At their nods, he went on. "We don't know a lot
about Binky. She was found as a stray on the west side of the city.
We think she was on her own for quite some time because she's a bit
underweight, and when she came in, her fur was very matted. She's
a Chihuahua mix, and we're estimating her age to be around five.
She needs some leash training, but we're working with her on that.
Overall, she's opinionated, but gentle."

"Like so many women I know," said Evan from behind them.
Keegan heard the sound of a smack and guessed Grace had let him
have it.

"Beckett was surrendered by his family." Here, Trent gave a

small sigh. "They had a baby and decided he was too big and they didn't have the time for him."

Keegan's heart ached.

"Oh, that poor boy," Sammi said, her voice quiet, her emotion clear.

"Yeah." Trent shook his head as he made a left. "He's a great dog. Gentle. Smart. Loving. He had a rough time adjusting to shelter life. His family was all he knew. He's only two, and he suffered some depression. But we've all been giving him love, and Lisa's been working on training him, and he's just a brilliant dog. Picks things up like that." He snapped his fingers, which Keegan couldn't really see in the dark but heard clearly. "He'll make somebody a fantastic companion."

The ride to the mall didn't take long, and within the next hour, they were inside at the gift wrapping site, which was situated in one of the kiosks in a high-traffic area. There they met Ingrid and Michelle, the women who were gift wrapping that night. A pen was set up so the dogs could be somewhat free. Beckett could probably have jumped it, Keegan noticed, but he didn't. He sat handsomely and watched as people came to shower Binky with attention.

The mall wasn't Keegan's favorite place in general, but at Christmas? Oh yes. She loved it. All the decorations made the entire place sparkle like it had been sprinkled with jewels—red, green, diamond. Several trees stood in the center of the walkway, super high, decorated in themes—all silver, all shoes, all dogs, all kitchen utensils. Whoever chose the themes had been super creative, and Keegan locked away the ideas to copy with her classes in the future. Holiday music was piped in through the PA, not loud, but constant. The entire feeling of the mall was one of festivity and joy, and she felt herself absorbing it all, standing a little taller, and feeling extra grateful to be there.

They got themselves situated, and Keegan was shocked by how quickly the line of people who needed things wrapped grew. Sammi stood next to her at the counter all four of them were using, cutting and taping, and Keegan was pretty sure she heard her mutter a curse.

When she glanced over, she blinked at the disaster of a reindeer-covered gift in front of her.

"Um, what are you doing?" Keegan asked quietly, amused.

"I'm wrapping. What does it look like I'm doing?" Sammi's tone said she knew she was terrible, and she lowered her voice to a whisper as she indicated Ingrid and Michelle with her eyes. "Those two do *not* mess around."

Keegan couldn't help but laugh softly, and she took the mess of wrapped gift from Sammi's hands. "How about you go hang out with the dogs and help Trent answer people's questions, and I'll wrap. Yeah?" Sammi seemed to try to make a disappointed face, which made Keegan laugh harder. "Oh, please. Don't even pretend you're not relieved."

"I am *so* relieved. You're the best." Then she kissed her quickly on the cheek and bolted from the booth, leaving Keegan standing there, feeling the warmth of the lip print on her face.

She watched as Sammi stepped into the pen, where she gave Beckett some love. His tail wagged, and he totally tuned in to her. It was super cute, and the way Sammi's face lit up was something to see. Sammi had also been right about Ingrid and Michelle. They did *not* mess around when it came to gift wrapping. Not only were they speedy quick, but the packages they wrapped were gorgeous, all neat, tidy corners and beautiful ribbons and bows. Keegan prided herself on her gift-wrapping prowess, but these women could teach her a thing or two or twelve. She sidled up to Michelle.

"Can you show me how you made that curlicue thing?"

"You bet," Michelle said with a smile.

Ingrid leaned across her. "That's her signature, the curlicue. I had her teach me, too."

After that, the three of them were fast friends.

Keegan wrapped what felt like a hundred gifts, all the while watching Sammi out of the corner of her eye. She was great with people, but also with the dogs, which didn't really come as a surprise. It wasn't long before Sammi was sitting on the floor in the pen with them, and Beckett was lying half in her lap. She petted his head as Keegan eavesdropped on her talking to one man about how important donations were to Junebug. The whole time, Evan was walking around, taking pictures of what seemed like anything and everything, and Keegan was curious to see what he'd end up with. Grace sat on a bench a few yards away taking notes on her phone and glancing around every so often, then jotting more notes.

By the time nine o'clock rolled around—the time their kiosk shut down, even though the mall was open until ten all through December—Keegan was dead on her feet. "Wow," she said as they started to put things away. "Teaching five-year-olds all day doesn't even compare to this."

Ingrid laughed. "It's not for the faint of heart. You should see it the last couple days before Christmas."

"Absolute chaos," Michelle filled in. "The number of people who wait until the last minute to do their shopping astounds me every year."

Keegan laughed and thanked them and wished them happy holidays. Then she moved to the dogs.

"How'd it go over here?" Keegan asked Sammi as Trent leashed the dogs, handed the leashes to Sammi, and began folding the pen up.

"Well, three families were interested in Binky here and filled out applications." She glanced down at the Chihuahua, who had finally settled. "Not a nibble on poor Beckett, though. People are so scared of dogs that look like him, and he's just a sweetheart." It bothered her. Keegan could see it in her eyes.

"That just means he's meant for somebody else," Keegan said and rubbed Beckett's velvety ear between her fingers.

By the time they got back to Junebug Farms, unloaded the dogs, and headed out to their cars, Keegan was yawning every few minutes.

"Wow," Sammi said when they'd reached Keegan's car. "I'm beat."

"Same." She glanced at her watch. Ten fifteen. "I'm usually already in bed by now. Kindergarteners show up with a lot of energy in the morning."

"I bet. My first appointment is at seven, so I feel you." They stood there for a moment, each looking off in different directions, until Sammi said, "Well, I guess our next thing is Saturday. See you then?"

"Sounds good." With a nod, Sammi headed for her car. Keegan opened her own car door, then turned back. "Hey, Sammi?"

"Yeah?"

"I had fun with you tonight."

She couldn't really see Sammi smile in the dark of the night, but she knew she did because she could hear it in her voice as she said, "Me, too."

Settled into her driver's seat, she started her car and blew out a long, slow breath and felt a little bit exhilarated, yes. A lot exhausted, definitely. But also…content. Very, very content.

She wasn't sure what to do with that.

CHAPTER SEVEN

*H*ey, *it's a gorgeous snowy evening, and I feel like walking. Wanna come with?*

It was after six on Thursday. There was a beautiful light snow falling, and the temperature hovered just around thirty degrees, as Sammi texted Chrissy, whose reply came back immediately.

Sure. Not like I have a date or anything exciting. Meet?

Sammi grinned. *Headed to Junebug Farms. Feel like walking dogs.*

The gray dots bounced, then Chrissy's response came through. *Seriously? Fine. Weirdo. See you there.*

There was something about this type of winter weather that had Sammi all up in her feels. Maybe it was the quiet. She'd read somewhere that snow absorbed sound, and that's why snowy days seemed quieter than summer ones. She liked that. Now, as she brushed off her car—the last one left in the parking lot of her office—she felt a silent relaxation come over her. Once her car was all clear of snow, she stood there, head tipped back, and just looked up at the huge expanse of deep sky, at the tops of the trees nearby, reaching up into that expanse, and at the big, fluffy flakes falling to the ground. It was all so beautiful, it took Sammi's breath away. She inhaled the cold, crisp air and held it in her lungs before letting it go.

The drive to Junebug didn't take long, and she was slipping into a spot in no time. It wasn't super busy, but there were a handful of cars sprinkled around hers, and inside, the lobby was humming with activity.

"You just missed your grandmother," the woman behind the desk told her with a smile.

"Did I?" Sammi hadn't talked to her grandma yet that day. "Bummer. Well, I'm here to walk a dog." She glanced at the front door where Chrissy was stomping her feet on the mat just inside. "And my friend here is, too."

Just a few moments later, they had leashes in hand and were choosing dogs to walk. Sammi breathed a quiet breath of relief when she found Beckett's kennel. "Hi, boy," she said quietly, and the dog's entire body shook with happiness and excitement. "Wanna go for a walk?"

Lisa had the keys, and when she came down the hall, she also had a green and black plaid dog coat. "He's short-haired, so let's put this on him for outside."

Chrissy had chosen a small terrier mix named Crisco, and soon the four of them were out in the snow. They walked in silence for a moment before Chrissy said, "Okay, I initially thought you were a little nuts wanting to randomly walk shelter dogs on a Thursday night, but this *is* kinda nice, not gonna lie."

"Right?"

"Also, I think that dog's in love with you." Chrissy gestured to Beckett, who was happy as could be trotting alongside Sammi, sniffing on occasion, but also glancing up at her regularly.

"Feeling's mutual. Huh, buddy?" She ruffled his ears, and he wagged his stump of a tail.

"You gonna adopt him? You should."

"Eh, I don't think so. My hours are crazy. I feel like it wouldn't be fair to leave him cooped up in the house all day."

"You mean as opposed to being cooped up in the shelter all day?"

Sammi snorted a laugh. "Valid."

"How did things go at the mall? I saw the posts online. The photos were so cool. And I still can't believe they ended up with two queens. How strange. And awesome." They followed the shoveled path that led from the main building toward the barn where the large farm animals were housed—horses, cows, sheep, and such. All were also up for adoption.

"It was fun, actually, though I suck at wrapping. Keegan saved me 'cause she's good at it. So she wrapped with the two ladies there who were, like, world class wrappers, oh my God." Chrissy laughed at her words and Sammi went on. "I'm serious. If gift wrapping was an Olympic sport, those women would have gold medals. It was fascinating and only served to shine a spotlight on just how terrible I am at it."

"Oh, I know. I've received gifts from you that look like a kindergartener wrapped them."

Sammi was laughing at this point. "I want to be shocked and appalled, but I also know you're right. Anyway, Keegan helped them wrap, and I talked to people about the shelter. Jessica said we got quite a few online donations that night, so that's good. And I'm pretty sure the other dog that was with us got adopted. I didn't see her in there."

"The other dog?"

"Yeah, we brought two. This guy and a little Chihuahua. Nobody even asked about Beckett, though."

"I mean, he's pretty intimidating to look at, with his barrel chest and giant block head."

Sammi feigned a gasp and comically covered Beckett's ears. "Don't you listen to her, sweetie. You're devastatingly handsome."

"And you were good hanging out with Keegan?" Chrissy shook her head as they rounded the barn to head back toward the main building. "Seriously, what are the freaking chances you'd end up not only with two queens, but that the other one would be her? It's such a ridiculous coincidence."

"Right? So weird. It was good, though. We had fun. We laughed a lot."

"When's the next gig?"

"Saturday. There's a dog bakery near the lake. We're making Christmas cookies."

"For dogs."

"Yep."

"Good thing you're a better baker than you are a wrapper."

"Hey, I can rap." And then she launched into a truly terrible rendition of Eminem's "Lose Yourself" until Chrissy was laughing so hard, her eyes teared up.

"Stop! Oh my God, stop, you're ruining the entire song for me."

They continued to follow the path around the barn and back, taking their time, letting the dogs sniff and explore.

Chrissy bounced on the balls of her feet as Crisco sniffed a bush. "I read once that letting a dog sniff all the things is equal to them walking for thirty minutes or something like that."

"I think I read that same article," Sammi said with a nod. "I get so irritated when I see people pulling their dogs along on walks. Let 'em sniff!"

"Right?" Crisco finally finished her inspection and moved along. "Hey, so, I have this friend who has a friend…"

"Oh, I hate the sound of this already," Sammi said, a soft laugh puffing out of her.

"Come on. She sounds really nice. When's the last time you were on a real date?"

Sammi sighed because it had actually been with Keegan. "Long time ago."

"Exactly. Plus, this could be a group thing instead of a date with just the two of you. Less pressure that way."

"I don't know…" She surprised herself when her brain started thinking logically. That was unusual, since she was a person who led with emotion. She groaned. "Fine. Tell me about her."

She felt more than saw Chrissy's head whip around in shock. "Seriously? That was easy."

"I didn't say I'd go. I said tell me about her."

"Okay, here's what I know…"

By the time Sammi was back in her car and headed home, she was scheduled to go to the Funhouse the next night in a group of six people, three of whom she knew and two she didn't. Including Sarah, the person Chrissy wanted her to meet. While she wouldn't say she was exactly looking forward to it, she wasn't dreading it, and in her mind right now, that was as good as it was going to get.

❖

The Funhouse was one of the newer hangouts in Northwood, and Keegan had only been once before, but she'd loved it. It had everything: bowling alleys, foosball tables, Ping-Pong, video games, air hockey, a bar, and a small restaurant. Definitely similar to a giant arcade for grownups. And now, all decked out for the holidays, it felt extra festive and shiny, with silver garland strung around windows and multicolored twinkle lights pretty much everywhere. Keegan loved it.

She'd wanted to do something different, and getting Jules to come had been more difficult than she'd expected. But she'd told her to invite a couple of her friends and they'd go as a group, so at seven thirty, four of them—Keegan, Jules, and two of Jules's work friends, Jason and Charice—had shoes and balls in hand and were headed for the bowling alleys.

Keegan loved to bowl. She'd been in a league when she was a kid and on into her early adulthood, way before she'd finished school and moved back to Northwood to teach. She hadn't taken the time to look for a league here, but picking up her sparkly red bowling ball felt like coming home, and when she took her first shot, flicking her wrist and sending the ball in a long, beautiful curve down the alley to level every pin but one, the silence that settled over her three friends was incredibly satisfying.

"Um, is your date a ringer, Jules?" Jason asked.

"It's news to me, but I'm thinking she might be," Jules said in response.

Keegan stifled a sigh. "I told you I bowled for years."

"You didn't tell me you were good."

"I am."

"I see that." Jules sipped her beer, her eyes never leaving Keegan.

Keegan shrugged and took a seat. Something she'd discovered

about Jules—she didn't pay a ton of attention because she was distracted a lot of the time, mostly by her phone. Case in point, Jason had to tell her three times that it was her turn.

Jules slid her phone into her back pocket and took her first shot. She just clipped the ten pin, and that was it. "When we're done here, I wanna play pinball," she said, taking her phone back out.

Jason and Charice were nice enough people, but they worked with Jules at the remodeling company, so the three of them talked a lot about that. People and situations Keegan was unfamiliar with, customers and other coworkers and vendors. She found herself smiling or laughing softly when it seemed appropriate, but she mostly didn't know what they were talking about.

"Who needs a refill?" she asked when she'd drained her own beer, and Jason requested a Bacardi and Coke. She strolled toward the bar, stopping to watch a Ping-Pong game for a moment, then what seemed like a very intense air hockey match between two college-aged guys who played like some kind of championship was on the line. Along the wall, the video games blinked and beeped, and she had a sudden burning desire to get some tokens and play *Ms. Pac-Man* until she couldn't feel her fingers. Maybe later.

The huge Christmas tree in the lobby was real, much to her surprise, and she admired it on her way to the bar. Very tall and nicely decorated, it reminded her that she needed to buy a new ornament for her own tree, which she did every year.

The bar was busy, and she bellied up to it and waited her turn, scanning the other patrons around the U-shaped counter. At thirty-three years old, she put herself right about in the middle as far as the age of the other customers went. There was a gaggle of girls to her left that seemed to be barely above the drinking age of twenty-one, very giggly. Past them was a pair of guys, probably in their late twenties. At one end of the U was what looked like a group of couples, late thirties, early forties, maybe? And next to them was a woman who was around her age, talking to another whose back was to Keegan. Hard to estimate an age from the back…And then she turned and Keegan could see her profile.

"Thirty-four," she said softly, as she recognized Sammi.

"Sorry?" The bartender stood in front of her, looking perplexed.

"Oh. I'm sorry. Um, yeah, can I get a Bacardi and Coke and a Heineken, please?"

"You got it."

Keegan hazarded a glance toward Sammi, who hadn't seen her. She was laughing. Not a soft, polite laugh, no. She was full-on *laughing* at something the other woman had said. Keegan didn't recognize her, but she was pretty. Blond, lean, not quite as tall as Sammi.

"Here you go, love." The bartender slid her order in front of her.

"Thanks." Keegan paid, picked up the drinks, and headed back toward the bowling alleys without saying hello, and if somebody had asked her why, she wouldn't have a logical answer. She felt like she was fleeing the scene.

Probably because she was.

❖

So? What did you think?

Chrissy's text pinged through Saturday morning, just as Sammi was getting out of the shower. She dried herself off, toweled her hair, combed it, and put in product before she texted back.

She was nice.

The gray dots bounced, and Sammi could picture Chrissy furiously typing out her irritated response. Sure enough, it popped through. *Nice? Nice? That's all you can come up with?*

She grinned at her own reflection because part of her was just messing with Chrissy. She'd actually liked Sarah more than she'd expected to. There was no reason not to. She was attractive, funny, successful. She'd made the evening much less awkward than Sammi had braced for, and she'd had a pretty great time.

That was, until she'd noticed Keegan at the bar. Seriously, what the hell was going on? They were suddenly popping up in each other's worlds on a shockingly regular basis. That was weird, right? She didn't know for sure if Keegan had seen her, but something in her gut told her Keegan had, and had chosen not to say anything. She wasn't sure if it was out of respect or hurt that she'd decided to also not say anything, and that had colored the rest of her night. She was pretty sure Sarah had felt her shift in attitude and must have wondered what she'd done to cause it. Sammi felt bad about that.

I had a good time, she texted, knowing it was still far from what Chrissy had hoped to hear.

Well, she liked you. A lot. She followed that up with about twenty-five heart eyes emoji, which made Sammi laugh. *How do you feel about another date?*

And there it was. The question she'd known was coming. "God, this is just stupid, isn't it?" she asked the woman in the mirror looking back at her. "It's just stupid. What is wrong with me?" Being stuck on Keegan was doing nothing good for her. And Keegan had made it pretty clear last year that it didn't work for her, that all she wanted was a friendship. Why she was so hung up on the woman was something Sammi had no explanation for.

She took in a deep, slow breath and spoke to her reflection. "Just get through this dog stuff," she whispered. "Just get through this dog stuff and then we'll keep our distance from her for a while. Maybe that'll do the trick." She studied her own eyes, saw the uncertainty in them, the hurt, the confusion. "Gah!" She tossed her towel. "Fine." She typed a text back to Chrissy.

Sure. Why not? I'll text her myself later.

Chrissy's response was to send every celebratory emoji there was, from the party horn to the red balloon. *Fantastic!*

She smiled and shook her head at Chrissy's vicarious joy. The conversation ended there, and Sammi got ready for her day at That Doggone Bakery. Her weather app told her it was going to be a cold and snowy day, so she chose jeans and a black sweater. As she finished drying her hair, her phone lit up on the counter. A text from her mother.

Grandma's making French toast...

"Say no more," Sammi murmured, finishing up, grabbing

her coat and boots. The weather app hadn't lied. Snow was falling steadily, and the plows had yet to come through, so she trudged across the street to her grandmother's house and stomped her way in through the side door.

"That didn't take long," her mother said with a soft laugh.

"You said French toast. What more do I need?" She hung her coat on the hook near the steps, toed off her boots, and entered the kitchen, which was warm and smelled like cinnamon. Soft holiday music came from the Bluetooth speaker on top of the fridge, and her grandma's Christmas towels were draped over the handle of the oven. A couple of festively dressed stuffed birds decorated the windowsill. The table was set for three. "Clearly, you knew I'd come."

"I've met you."

Sammi grinned and gave her mom a kiss, then moved to the counter where her grandmother manned the electric frying pan and kissed her as well.

"Do they even make these things anymore, Grams?" she asked, indicating the pan.

Her grandma frowned. "You know what? I have no idea." She used her spatula to flip the four slices of French toast, revealing golden brown goodness. Sammi's mouth watered. "You've got the bakery today?"

"Yup. At noon. I think we're actually gonna bake, too."

"That sounds fun," her mother said, getting syrup and butter from the fridge. "I think we're gonna stop by."

"Yeah?"

"We've got some errands to run, so we'll just add you to the list."

Sammi spent the next hour chatting with her family and eating breakfast. She had yet to find any restaurant in Northwood with better French toast than her grandmother's, and she told her so every time she made it. Her grandma also blushed every time.

By the time eleven thirty rolled around, she was pulling her SUV into the parking lot at Junebug Farms. Snow had continued to fall steadily, but it was fluffy and light and generally just blew out of the way. Not too bad for driving, at least so far. But winter weather could change in a heartbeat and become treacherous. Hopefully, not today.

Keegan was already there—Sammi had seen her car in the lot—and her heart skipped a beat, as usual. She sighed, wondering how she could get that to stop. Maybe taking Sarah out would do the trick. She glanced around as she crossed the lobby to the desk where Keegan, Grace, and Evan all were. Interestingly, no Jules. Again.

"Hey," she said, as Keegan met her gaze and smiled widely, as if happy to see her.

"Hi, you. How's your Saturday so far?" Keegan asked.

"Well, I've got a belly full of French toast, and I'm about to hang out with some dogs and make some dog treats, so I gotta say, it's not a bad one."

"Oh, I'm jealous of the French toast," Keegan said, feigning a pout. "All I had was a Pop-Tart. Unfrosted."

Sammi gasped. "Unfrosted? That's just a travesty."

"Tell me about it. I bought them by accident."

"You poor thing. You have my sympathy."

Lisa came out from the dog wing then, with two dogs on leashes. She greeted them with a warm smile. "You guys have done great so far. We've gotten several large donations, and Binky was adopted by a family in the mall that night."

"Not Beckett?" Sammi asked.

Lisa shook her head. "Not yet." She handed over one leash to Sammi. "This is Belle. She's a Lab mix, about two, found as a stray." Belle's entire yellow body wagged along with her tail. She looked up at Sammi with big brown eyes and sat. Lisa laughed. "Yeah, she's not gonna last long." She handed the other leash to Keegan. "This is Ralphie. He's an older guy whose owner passed away suddenly. He's been a little depressed, but he's coming out of his shell. He's a pug mix." Ralphie was all wrinkled tan skin and squished nose. His body was rotund—his owner had clearly fed him well—and there was an air of sadness around him.

Sammi watched as Keegan squatted down so she was close

to his face. She whispered something to him Sammi couldn't hear, then petted him tenderly and stood up.

"Trent's pulling the van around," Lisa said. "Anybody have any questions?" When heads shook all around, she pretended to wave them away. "Good. You're gonna love this place. Go! Make all the cookies. Tell Makenna I said hi." The group headed for the exit.

❖

That Doggone Bakery had been in business for nearly ten years. Keegan had done some research in preparation for her day there. Makenna Covington was the owner, and she'd started it in her own kitchen, surprised when it had exploded into success. She kept her name and the name of her shop in the forefront of people's minds by sponsoring teams, donating treats to shelters, and hosting adoption days there. Keegan had never met her but liked her instantly just from what she'd read.

"I think we'll do things pretty much the same way we did at the mall," Grace was saying, pulling Keegan back into the moment. "You guys just do what you're gonna do. Evan will take photos. I'll post on socials. Just ignore us, yeah?"

Sammi nodded, absently stroking Belle's head as Sammi looked out the window, as they'd forgone the crates for this ride. Sammi was quiet today, Keegan noticed. A bit distant. And even as she wondered what might be on her mind, she appreciated what she'd worn. The jeans looked soft and worn, slightly threadbare around one knee. Under the Junebug fleece, her black sweater only accentuated her dark features, and its V-neck shifted every so often to offer Keegan a tiny glimpse of what might lie beneath it.

She groaned internally. *Stop it.* As always, being this close to Sammi had her blood racing, and she looked away, gazed out the window with Ralphie on her lap.

"I really like you guys," Trent said from the driver's seat, his voice sounding loud to Keegan's quieting mind.

"Well, we like you too, Trent," Sammi said with a grin.

"No, I mean, we have crates in the back of the van. The dogs are usually there for rides. But I like that you two wanted the dogs to be next to you. It's very cool."

Keegan glanced at Sammi, who was looking her way, and smiled. God, those dark and stormy eyes of hers made Keegan want to dive into them…But she remembered how scary that had been last time, how she'd balked. *Too much. Too much.* She cleared her throat. "I can't speak for Sammi, but I just want these dogs to get as much love and as many pets as they can. They spend enough of their day in a cage, you know?"

Sammi nodded. "Same."

"Well, I think it's cool," Trent said again, his smiling eyes meeting Keegan's in the rearview mirror. "I'm glad we went with two queens."

"Yeah," Grace said, leaning forward in her seat so her head was between Keegan and Sammi. "How *did* that happen?"

Sammi shrugged as Keegan shook her head. "We have no idea. You'd have to ask Jessica. She's in charge."

That Doggone Bakery was in a small building tucked between a bookstore and a coffee shop along the retail strip of Black Cherry Lake. The outside was painted a bright blue, and the window display featured two stuffed dogs sitting at a round table, a third dog in a chef's hat and apron serving them goodies from a tray. Trent stopped the van along the street, and the group unloaded, then he drove it to the parking lot.

The front door pushed open and a very attractive brunette greeted them with a smile. She wore a blue and white hat with the bakery's logo on it, her dark ponytail hanging out the back. "Hi there! You must be the gang from Junebug Farms." And then, without waiting for a response, she dropped down into a squat and gave all her attention to the dogs. "Well hello. Hello there. Hello there. How are you? You're so pretty, ma'am. Yes, you are. And you, sir? Very handsome. So handsome. Are you good dogs? Yeah? Do you want some treats? Do you? Yeah? Come on in."

Keegan and Sammi exchanged glances. Oh, this was going to be a fun day.

They headed inside, as the snow had started to blow. The shop was quite small, but also cozy and inviting. A small Christmas tree stood in the corner, lit up in green and red lights, and decorated with dog ornaments and bone-shaped cookie cutters. There were glass display cases, just like any regular bakery, trimmed in white twinkle lights, and the kitchen in the back was fully open and visible.

"It might be a bit of a tight squeeze," Makenna said, her eyes smiling. "It's not a big place, but we can manage, right?"

Evan was already snapping photos of the shop, and he actually went back outside and took some shots through the window. Belle had her nose pressed against a glass display case, and Ralphie pawed at Keegan's leg until she picked him up. His center of gravity was so low, she groaned with effort. "God, you're like picking up a cinder block, buddy."

He licked her face in response.

"This is great, what you guys are doing," Makenna said. There was an old-timey swinging door between the display cases, and she held it open after she passed through. "Come on back, and we'll get baking."

Sammi looked around the shop as she held up Belle's leash. "What should we do with...?"

"Bring 'em back," Makenna said, her voice filled with cheer. "They can taste test. I usually have my boys back here with me, but I knew you were coming, so I left them home today. I thought four dogs in the kitchen might be a bit much." Her laugh was musical and contagious, and it made Keegan grin. "Normally, it'd be a big no-no to have them back here, but I don't have the same government regulations around my kitchen because I'm not making food for humans." She pointed to some hooks on the far wall. "Grab a couple aprons, and we'll get to work." She picked up her phone and made some selections, and then Taylor Swift was singing about calming down, her voice emanating from a speaker Keegan couldn't see.

There were lots of ingredients on shelves, including big tubs of peanut butter, large containers of oats, a basket of sweet potatoes, and several bunches of bananas. There was a refrigerator next to a big, stainless steel counter. A hanging basket held countless cookie cutters, and there were two food processors on another counter next to a large oven.

She glanced at Sammi, who had tied on a black apron like a pro. She'd pulled her hair back and fastened it with a hair clip she'd apparently pulled out of thin air. Evan took a few shots of her, probably because she looked super hot in that moment, a fact that wasn't lost on Keegan.

"Okay," Sammi said with a clap of her hands. "What are we making?"

Makenna had a great smile, almost as compelling as her laugh, all white teeth and dimples. Something about her…she just seemed to emanate happiness. Keegan didn't know very many people like that, but she liked being around Makenna Covington.

"I thought we'd stick to some simple stuff. The fewer ingredients the better for dog treats, so I thought we'd make some peanut butter banana ones and some cheddar bacon ones. Sound good?"

For the next three hours, they baked. They scooped and mixed and rolled and cut and drizzled and frosted, and it was the most fun Keegan had had in a long, long time. She and Sammi worked side by side, their hips bumping, their shoulders brushing. Sammi smelled like raspberries and cream for some reason.

"Did you wash your hair in fruit?" she finally asked, when they'd had enough of those bumps and brushes that she felt comfortable teasing.

"I did, yes," Sammi said, without missing a beat. She was rolling out some peanut butter banana oat dough and didn't look up. "Every morning, I mash up a bushel of raspberries and then stick my head in it."

Keegan laughed softly. "Well, it smells really nice."

Sammi looked at her then. She could feel it. "Thanks."

Only then did it occur to Keegan just how close everybody was and that they'd likely heard the whole exchange. A glance around showed her both Evan and Grace looking intently at their phones, though Grace seemed to be stifling a smile.

"You two are so cute," Makenna said with a knowing look. "How long have you been together?"

Keegan felt her cheeks heat up. "Oh, um, we're not…" She shook her head.

"No?" Makenna's eyes went wide. "Wow. I'm so sorry. I'm shocked. I'm usually really good at picking up on that kind of thing." She made a yikes face. "I'm really sorry."

"Don't be," Sammi said. "I could do way worse." And she bumped Keegan again but kept her eyes on her dough.

"Facts," Evan chimed in from his corner, where he was shooting a wide shot, and made them all laugh.

Several times as they worked, customers would come in with their dogs, the sleigh bells hanging from the door jingling merrily. Belle and Ralphie would get excited, Belle's tail sweeping things off countertops and whacking shins. Makenna lit up like the proverbial Christmas tree every time. She knew many of the people by name and pretty much all the dogs, and Keegan thought it was so cute how she got down to dog level every time so she was speaking directly to them.

At one point, Sammi's grandma and mom came through the door, and the way Sammi's entire demeanor shifted to obvious joy at seeing them was something to behold. They waved at Keegan and didn't stay long but were clearly thrilled to see Sammi in an apron in the kitchen.

"You two having a good time?" Mia asked, a knowing tone of some sort in her voice.

Keegan nodded, as did Sammi, who then said, "Yes, and we're working, so stop bothering us." But her tone was light and held no irritation. She was kidding.

Sammi's mom and grandma both bought several bags of treats, even though they didn't have dogs, and Keegan thought that was super kind of them. Then they waved some more and headed back out into the snow.

Keegan decided she loved it there at That Doggone Bakery. She found herself disappointed she only had cats, as she wanted to come back and visit often. Makenna's cheerful disposition, the warmth and coziness of the shop, the creativity of her treats, the way the customers seemed to fill with joy when they entered, along with the cheerfulness of the Christmas decorations, not to mention the surprisingly delicious smells, made it a place she found herself taking comfort in. Unexpected, that.

Belle loved everything they made, though she seemed most fond of the bacon-glazed peanut butter treats. Ralphie turned up his smooshy nose at the majority of the treats, which was kind of hilarious, but Makenna wouldn't stop, and she won him over with a chicken and rice treat she pulled from the display case. "Pugs, man," she said with a good-natured shake of her head. Then she packed up a bag of them for Ralphie and a variety for Belle.

Keegan didn't want to leave. The thought had only just crossed her mind when Sammi said, "I love it here. I want to live here."

"Me, too." Keegan smiled at her. "Hey, Makenna, is there room back there for cots? We've decided we don't want to leave."

"I have one already, but I'd happily invest in bunk beds."

"Deal," Keegan said. "I'll just go home and pack a bag."

Makenna surprised Keegan by throwing her arms around her and hugging her tight. Then she did the same to Sammi, then Evan and Grace and even Trent, when he'd parked the van out front. "I am so happy I got to meet you all. This was a great day." As was Makenna's way, Keegan understood after spending the afternoon with her, she then squatted down to speak with Ralphie and Belle. "And you two are such good doggies. You're gonna find forever homes soon, I just know it. Be good, okay?" She gave them both tender kisses on their furry heads, and Keegan found herself tearing up.

My God, who is this woman?

The ride back to Junebug was unexpectedly quiet. Keegan found herself in her own head, and all up in her feels after spending the day with somebody as loving and open about it as Makenna Covington.

"You okay?" Sammi asked quietly as they drove.

Keegan nodded. "I am. I just..." She searched for the right words to describe what she was feeling. "There was something about her, right?"

"Who? Makenna?" Sammi asked. At Keegan's nod, she chuckled. "Oh my God, yes."

"It was her aura or something," Grace said from the passenger seat in front of them.

"Yes," Keegan agreed with enthusiasm. "Not that I can see those. Or understand what they are exactly, but *something* about her makes me want to be better."

"Better than what?" Sammi asked.

"Better than who I usually am. Like, a better person."

"But you're already amazing. How much better do you want to be?"

Keegan met her gaze. The interior of the van was dim, dusk having settled during the ride. Sammi's expression was sincere, and Keegan felt an almost irresistible urge to lean into her, to press her lips to Sammi's, but she managed to keep control of herself. "Thank you," she said on a whisper. "You're sweet."

"True. But I'm also right," Sammi said with a smile, then turned her gaze back toward the window.

Chapter Eight

It had snowed steadily overnight and was still coming down as Mia drove herself to Junebug Farms. Maggie had begged her not to go. Her daughter-in-law worried so much about her these days, and while Mia did appreciate the concern, she did not enjoy being made to feel like a feeble old woman. Yes, she was eighty. So what? She was much more active than most eighty-year-olds she knew. There were aches and pains, of course. Your body didn't survive eighty years of living without some of those. But she was not an invalid. She was not a frail woman who needed to be carted all over the place. She'd hired a plow guy to make sure her driveway was clear, and she'd bought herself a four-wheel-drive SUV so she wouldn't slip-slide away down the road. She'd lived in Northwood, New York, all her life. A little snow didn't scare her.

Apparently, it scared a lot of other people, though, judging by the lack of cars in the parking lot. She recognized Jessica's Toyota—of course she was there. Mia was fairly certain she'd slept there on occasion on the couch in her office. Thank goodness she had Sydney to hopefully keep it from happening too often. She parked and trudged to the front door. One of the handymen was shoveling the walkways and tossing pet-safe ice melt on them.

"Morning, James," she said with a wave.

"Mrs. Sorenson," he greeted back, and she shook her head, deciding not to gently berate him for the nine hundredth time to call her Mia. Another fact of old age—nobody addressed her by her first name anymore.

She stomped the snow off her boots, then waved to the one woman already behind the reception desk as she passed by and headed into the volunteer break room, which was empty. It was unusual for it to be so quiet there. Even the dogs seemed to be barking at a slightly lower volume than normal. She hung up her coat, fluffed her hair, then went in search of Lisa so she could help feed the dogs their breakfast. She might even peek in on the cats today, too, she decided. While she wasn't as drawn to the felines as she was to the dogs, she did like to pop into their wing, say hi, maybe cuddle a kitten or two, or an older cat who was struggling.

The dog wing was a long stretch, with a visitation room on the immediate right and then kennels on either side. About halfway down was Lisa's desk and workspace, and as Mia headed in that direction, she saw Jessica was there as well, the two women chatting.

"Mia," Jessica said with a smile as she looked up. "Come look at these." She had her phone out and was scrolling with her thumb. "It looks like Saturday went great." She handed Mia her phone.

The screen showed several shots of Sammi and Keegan at the dog bakery. "Oh my goodness," she said. The first thing she noticed was how happy Sammi looked, a fact she recalled from her short visit to the bakery. She supposed if you didn't know Sammi and were looking at the photos, she just looked like a normal smiling person. But Mia knew that face inside and out, and she could tell Sammi was ecstatic. The funny thing was, Keegan had the same look. There were several shots of them, the dogs always included. They were laughing, baking, feeding treats to the shelter dogs as well as to dogs Mia assumed were customers of the bakery. And there was one photo, the last one, that snagged Mia's eye and wouldn't let go. Sammi and Keegan were in profile, looking at each other and laughing. It seemed like they might not have realized the shot had been captured. Sammi's eyes were sparkling, and Mia had never seen Keegan's smile look so genuine.

They looked like they were in love.

"Two queens was a fantastic idea," Lisa said, yanking Mia back to the dog wing. "That was you?"

Mia lifted one shoulder. "I just counted votes."

Jessica put an arm around her shoulders and gave her a gentle squeeze. "Mia here helped me see that a little progressive controversy might get us more attention. And she wasn't wrong."

"Has any of it been bad attention?" Lisa asked with a grimace.

"Very little," Jessica said. "A couple of emails here and there. What is this world coming to when even the local shelter is pushing the *gay agenda*?" She rolled her eyes.

"What does that even mean?" Mia asked. "I mean that sincerely. I assume your gay agenda"—she pointed to Jessica—"is to find as many homes for these animals as you can. And yours"—she pointed at Lisa, for she knew Lisa was also married to a woman—"is to make sure they're fed and comfortable and loved while they're here. Sammi's is to be the best dentist she can be and also be a loving human. I just don't understand the anger." She shook her head, baffled, and Jessica hugged her more tightly.

"If only every person, young or old, thought like you, my friend. You are a treasure. You know that, right?" And when Mia glanced up at her, there were tears in Jessica's eyes.

"Oh, goodness, don't you go crying on me," she said with a soft laugh, and she hugged Jessica back. "I sometimes think I could use a wife myself." The laughter was shared, and Mia added, "It takes special people to do what you two do. I'm honored to be able to help in any way I can."

"Well, we're lucky to have you," Jessica said. "I hope you know how much we appreciate all you do here. I know we get so busy and caught up in stuff and sometimes take you for granted, but I need you to know how valuable you are to us here. Thank you, Mia."

Mia held her gaze and gave a gentle nod. A beat passed, and she clapped her hands once. "Okay. Enough of this blubbering. What can I do?"

Ten minutes later, she was helping to feed several of the dogs. The shelter was nearly full, which was never good. But more donations had come through in the past week, and at least the stockpile of kibble had been replenished. It wouldn't last long, given the number of dogs, but for now, they all had enough.

Knowing food was coming woke up the noise level, that was for sure. On occasion, Mia wore earplugs when she worked inside, but she'd forgotten them today, and the sound was piercing. Two tiny Chihuahuas that were found as strays and were a bonded pair had such high-pitched barks, they made Mia cringe as she approached them. But she spoke to them in a soothing tone as she set down bowls, and soon they calmed down. Luckily, they were more interested in breakfast than in nipping at her hands. She went down the line and fed the dogs in six kennels in a row while Lisa worked on the other side of the hall. Her last one was Hulk, and when she got to him, her heart cracked a little.

He was lying on the little cot in the corner. His eyes moved to watch her approach, and his nub of a tail moved slightly in a half-hearted wag, but he didn't get up. Mia had volunteered there long enough to know the signs of depression in a dog, and she swallowed hard. Pulling the kennel door closed behind her, she went into the kennel with her bowl of kibble and lowered herself down to the floor—not an easy task at eighty. Hulk's cot was only a few inches high, just enough to keep him from lying on the cold cement, and he had a donated blanket underneath his solid body.

"Hi there, handsome," Mia said softly and stroked his big block-shaped head, the white hair on his chin sparkling a bit when it caught the overhead lights. "You don't look so happy this morning. You want some breakfast?" She held the bowl near his nose, and it twitched and he sniffed, but he didn't lift his head. "That's okay. I'll just hold it in case you change your mind." She set the bowl in her lap and scooted closer so she could put her arm around him.

She did that often, sat with a depressed dog. It allowed them to feel human companionship and love—things some of them had never really known—and she often found herself able to tune out the rest of the noise of the shelter and focus on whatever was on her mind that day.

Today? It was Sammi. Well, Sammi and Keegan.

Those photos. Good Lord.

She shook her head as she replayed them in her mind. Then she slid her own phone out of her pocket and opened Instagram so she could look at them more closely and in private.

There were several shots of each woman individually. Baking, stroking the dog they brought, chatting with other customers, feeding a treat to a dog. In all of them, Sammi looked ridiculously happy. Mia knew her granddaughter well, and she knew her emotions. Sammi tried to hide them sometimes, but she couldn't hide them from Mia. And in these photos? She was filled with joy.

She didn't know Keegan well at all, but if she had to guess just from what she saw in the posts, Keegan had had a fantastic time as well.

It was that last shot, though, the one of the two of them looking at each other. She wondered again if they'd even known it was being taken. The photographer was behind them as they stood at the counter. Sammi was rolling out dough, and Keegan had a bone-shaped cookie cutter in her hand. They were looking at each other, Keegan slightly taller, her auburn hair pulled back into a haphazard ponytail, and they weren't smiling. They were clearly laughing, mouths open, eyes crinkled at the corners, the happiness just radiating off them, even in a photo on the screen of her phone, and Mia had never been more sure that there was something there. Love? Something close. Definitely.

"What do you think, big guy?" She turned the phone so Hulk could see the pictures. "Don't they look like they belong together?" Hulk's eyes moved over the screen, as if he was really taking it in. She lowered her voice as she stroked his head. "I didn't meddle, not really. I just pointed out the facts to Jessica. That's all. She might not have realized them if I hadn't."

Hulk looked up at her then, his soulful brown eyes almost human, and seemed to take her in.

"What?" she asked him.

He nudged the bowl on her lap.

"Oh, you want to try a little breakfast?" She scooped some

kibble into her hand and moved it to him. He, ever so gently, ate it from her palm, and they did this until he'd eaten the entire bowl. "How's that? Better? You feeling okay?"

He sighed, a deep, from the depths of his body, sigh.

"I know, sweetheart. It's kind of yucky out, but do you want to go for a walk? Maybe the fresh air will help, too."

Hulk seemed to think it over for a bit before rising slowly to his feet and stepping off the cot. He looked at her with expectation.

"A walk it is." She pushed to her feet.

❖

It was just over two weeks until Christmas—and less than two weeks until Christmas break—and you could feel it throughout the school.

Her kindergarteners were bouncing off the walls, which was typical for December. Christmas, Hanukkah, Kwanzaa, all of it added up to small kids filled with excitement. They were loud. They had short little fuses and more energy than Keegan thought she'd ever had in her entire life. Madness, that was December.

But she loved it.

Well, she loved it when she didn't feel like she wanted to lie down and take a nap. She was definitely coming down with something—drawback of working in a school, truly.

But she'd never wanted to be anything but a teacher, so she rarely complained. And she rarely scolded. She knew the kids mostly couldn't help their own adrenaline. They were five and six years old. It had taken her a couple years of teaching this age before she understood that by the end of the day, they were just done trying to learn. Their little brains had had enough. She usually took those last thirty or forty minutes and let them play, as they were doing now.

And yeah, she was now sure her annual winter cold was preparing to make its entrance. Her ears felt a bit like they were stuffed with cotton, and she'd sneezed about a dozen times already, and it all seemed to be intensifying as she stood there. The joys of being surrounded by small children all day, wiping their noses on their hands or sneezing directly into her eyeballs.

She wandered the room, making sure to break up any potential arguments or to give a quick lesson on sharing, but she mostly had a good group of little ones this year. And because they seemed to be having few issues that afternoon, she was able to let her mind drift a bit...back to Saturday at the dog bakery.

Which was no surprise. She'd pretty much spent her entire Sunday flashing back to different pieces and parts of it, so much so that Jules had asked her three times if she was okay.

No. No, she wasn't okay. Not at all.

She'd pulled away from Sammi for a reason—so she could focus on Jules—and she was failing miserably at that.

You're already amazing. How much better do you want to be?

Sammi's words had been echoing through her mind for the better part of thirty-six hours now. Had anybody ever said anything so kind? So genuine? With no expectation of anything in return? Not Jules, that's for sure. Ever since she'd balked at being referred to as Jules's girlfriend, Jules had been cooler, a bit more distant.

She also couldn't help but return to Makenna Covington's assumption that they were together. Not just together, but that they had been for a while. She seemed to be a really observant person, and the fact that she looked at the two of them and saw a couple, that was...interesting, wasn't it?

She couldn't remember the last time she'd had so much fun with somebody—on a date or not—as she had with Sammi at the dog bakery. They'd made what seemed like a ton of dog treats. They'd greeted customers as they came in and spoken to several of them about the dogs they had with them. She hoped they'd garnered some more donations for Junebug Farms. And the whole time, she'd felt a slow, soft buzzing in her body whenever she was next to Sammi, a thing she'd ignored—or tried to—the entire day. But it had been there. She could almost feel it now, just from reminiscing.

"I had it first!"

The frustrated little boy shout yanked her rudely back to the present, and she broke up a fight before it got out of control, giving yet another lesson on the importance of sharing.

Not long after that, her classroom was blissfully empty, and she sat at her desk in silence, legs crossed, elbow on the arm of her chair supporting her head. Her phone pinged an incoming text.

Still on for dinner?

Jules. She sighed, not quite sure why she just didn't want to deal with her tonight. She contemplated for a moment, then typed a response, because going out to dinner in a public place where there was noise and cold and other people was not tempting. Not even a little bit.

Rough day. Coming down with something. Not feeling great. Just gonna go home and pile. Rain check?

She hit send and felt immediately guilty, even though she wasn't lying. And she wasn't sure if she hoped Jules would come over and pamper her or if she'd rather she didn't.

Bummer. Well, I don't want to get sick, so text you later. Feel better.

"Ah, so warm and loving," Keegan said, then tossed her phone onto her desk in annoyance and immediately sneezed. "Damn it."

By the time she got home, out of her work outfit, and into comfy clothes, she felt like death. She took her sweats-clad self to the living room and collapsed onto the couch. Her cats were curious. Cocoa wandered around near her stomach and touched her face with his cold nose and tickly whiskers while Bean curled up between her feet, his purring vibrating along her legs. She was just dozing off when her phone announced a text. Jules changing her mind?

She smiled as she saw it was a text from Sammi.

Just thinking about you. Wanted to say hi and see if you're ready for training class tomorrow. Followed by a couple smiling emoji.

She typed back, *Hi! Not sure about tomorrow. I think the winter crud got me...* She added an emoji with a thermometer in its mouth and clicked send.

And then her phone rang in her hand. Sammi was calling. Her heart rate picked up noticeably.

"Who is this and how did you get this number?" she said as a joke when she answered, then immediately fell into a fit of coughing.

"Oh my God, you sound awful," Sammi said. "Do you have a fever?"

Keegan put a hand to her forehead, knowing it was hard to diagnose a fever on yourself. "Not sure. No chills, so maybe not?"

"You have water? Orange juice? Chicken soup?"

Seriously, how cute was she? "Yes. No. No."

"Well, you are very bad at being prepared for sickness." Sammi laughed softly. Her voice changed slightly when she said, "Jules taking care of you?"

Keegan didn't mean to snort, but she did anyway. "No, she is steering clear of my kid crud, apparently."

Did Sammi sigh? She was pretty sure she heard her sigh. "Can I do anything for you? Bring you anything?"

"You are very sweet." It was the truth, and Keegan stroked Cocoa's soft head as she said, "I'm just going to lie here on my couch. If you don't hear from me in, say, a week or so, maybe send somebody in to make sure my cats haven't eaten me completely. My mom will want something to bury."

Sammi's laugh was adorable as she answered, "You got it. Don't worry about tomorrow. It's just training class. I can do it alone. You get better because what I do *not* want to do alone is sing Christmas carols at the nursing home this weekend. Trust me, nobody wants that." They laughed a bit more, and then Sammi's voice went softer. "You sure you don't need anything?"

Keegan had a running list of things in her head she needed: some soup, some tea, maybe a little hot chocolate later, some Tylenol, a new box of tissues, the remote, which was about three feet away from her hand instead of two inches and would take effort to reach, somebody to rub her head and make her feel better... But all she said, very softly, was, "No, I'm okay. But thank you. I appreciate it."

They said their good-byes, and Keegan managed to stretch just far enough to reach the remote. She considered that a huge accomplishment, and now she was exhausted. She turned on the

TV to reruns of *Modern Family* and was asleep before she even registered which episode it was.

❖

Knock, knock!

Keegan jerked awake, momentarily confused by where she was, who she was, what the hell day it was. Which planet was this?

Knock, knock, knock!

She blinked rapidly in the ethereal blue glow of the television and the soft color of the Christmas tree lights, which made up the only light in her living room. She was weighed down by cats. Was somebody knocking at her door?

With a groan, she pushed herself to a sitting position, then had to wait a second for the wave of nausea to pass. Oh yeah, she was definitely sick. Full-blown. She swallowed several times until she felt like she could move safely.

The knocking came again, but a bit lighter this time, as if instead of getting more insistent, the knocker was becoming less sure of themselves. A glance at her phone told her it was just after seven o'clock. She'd been crashed out on her sofa for more than two hours.

She got to her feet, crossed the room, and didn't even look through the peephole. Just yanked the door open with what little irritation she could muster, and then gasped. Loudly.

"Sammi?"

"Hey, hi. Um, I hope this is okay." She clenched her teeth and grimaced. "I hated the idea of you being sick and alone, so"—she held up the two grocery bags Keegan now noticed in her hands—"I brought some stuff for you." Sammi glanced over her shoulder. "One of your neighbors came in the main door of the building, so I kind of piggybacked. I didn't know how obnoxious your buzzer might be."

If she hadn't been sick, Keegan would've been able to hide her reaction better. She knew that. But she was sick, and that meant her coping skills were low, and much to her horror, her eyes welled up. "You brought me stuff?"

"I did. Can I...?" Sammi gestured past Keegan with her eyes.

"Oh God, of course." She stepped aside. "Come in. Please." Sammi walked past her, smelling like snowfall and the outdoors, fresh and clean and comforting.

When she'd found the kitchen, Sammi put the bags up on the counter. "Okay." She began taking things out of them. "We've got some homemade chicken soup. I took it out of my freezer after I spoke with you earlier, but it hasn't quite thawed. Where are your pots?"

Keegan stood in the doorway, leaning against the doorjamb, and pointed. Sammi found a soup pot and set it on the stove. Then she crossed the room and laid her cool hand against Keegan's forehead.

"Oh yeah, you're running a fever. Let's get you back down."

Keegan let herself be led back to the couch where Sammi covered her with the blanket she'd been using, then grabbed another off the back of a chair. Her body started to shiver then, and she knew Sammi was right.

"Have you taken anything?" Sammi asked.

With a shake of her head, she said, "I fell asleep right after I spoke with you."

A nod, and Sammi disappeared into the kitchen, only to return with a glass of water and some Tylenol. "This will help with the fever. I'm going to warm you up some soup." She took the water back and tucked the blankets around Keegan. "Just relax, okay? You need rest. Best thing for you right now. Rest and fluids."

Keegan watched her return to the kitchen. She didn't need this. She didn't need any of it. She'd been sick plenty of times—you couldn't work in a school and not catch just about everything that went around—and she'd been sick plenty of times on her own. She could take care of herself. She always had. She was used to it.

But the sound of Sammi puttering around in her kitchen? The clicking of the burner being lit on the stove? The scrape of the spoon against the bottom of the pan? The warmth of somebody else in her space with her, doing things to make her feel less sick and less alone? Yeah, those were things she was *not* used to.

And how much she didn't want Sammi to leave? She was not used to that, either.

Her instinct was to get up and help. Having another person in her kitchen cooking while she lay on the couch like a useless sloth was not okay with her. But whatever she had must've settled in and made itself at home while she'd napped because—right now?—her legs felt like they were made of lead, and something in her brain told her that if she tried to move, her aching head would simply implode. The end.

She stayed on the couch.

Drifting in and out was a thing, apparently, because next time she opened her eyes, her water had been refilled, and next to it was a bottle of Gatorade. A new episode of *Modern Family* was on. God, had she ever been this tired before?

"Here we go." Sammi came in from the kitchen carrying a plate with a bowl in the middle. "I know you might not be hungry enough for the sandwich, but at least eat the soup." She set the plate down. A bowl of the chicken soup Sammi'd brought and a grilled cheese sandwich sat there in lovely presentation.

"Oh, Sammi, this…" She shook her head, honestly moved by everything Sammi was doing. "You didn't have to do this."

Sammi half shrugged. "I wanted to. When you're sick, you don't have the energy to get up and make yourself food, but you need to eat at least a little something."

She was hungry. The nausea had passed, and she felt like she could eat some of the soup, so she pushed herself to a sitting position and tasted it. "Oh my God."

"I know, right?" Sammi said with a smile. "My grandma makes kick-ass chicken soup. There's always a couple bowls in my freezer."

They sat in companionable silence for a bit, watching TV as Keegan ate every last drop of the soup, surprising herself. "Aren't you eating?" she asked when she'd finished, realizing Sammi had no food.

"I will." Sammi's smile was soft. "How's it sitting?" She indicated the soup bowl with her eyes.

"Okay so far."

"Good." Sammi stood up and gestured for her to lie back down. "Get comfortable." Then a thought seemed to occur to her and she stopped. "Would you rather be in bed?"

Keegan shook her head. "No, this is good."

"Okay." Sammi helped her get all situated, blankets tucked, liquids nearby. "Be back in a bit." With a grin, she took a bite of the uneaten sandwich, and then she gathered all the dishes together and disappeared into the kitchen. A minute or two later, Keegan could hear the water running and dishes being washed, and there was something so comforting and domestic and wonderful about it that she felt everything in her body settle. Despite her pounding head and her body aches and the fever she still had, judging by the chills that vibrated through her body at regular intervals, she felt utterly content. More than that, she was almost happy. She burrowed down into the couch.

The next time she opened her eyes, it was fully dark, except for the TV and the Christmas tree. And how was it possible to feel like death warmed over and also be super cozy and comfortable? It took a moment for her brain to start firing on all cylinders—or most of them, anyway—and that's when she realized she was lying up against a warm body. One that was way too big to be a cat. Yeah, she was pretty sure those were firm breasts pillowing her head. She glanced around without moving. Cocoa was on the chair across the room, a ball of fur curled up on Sammi's coat. Bean was stretched out on the back of the couch. She swallowed, cleared her throat, and pushed herself up so she could turn and look into Sammi's eyes.

Sammi was blinking rapidly, and Keegan felt her body shift and tense underneath her, as if Sammi was stretching without actually *stretching*. Keegan's expression must have held a question because Sammi looked sheepish for a moment before she said, "You asked me to stay." A chuckle. "Pretty sure it was your fever, but…" She shrugged as if to say *What was I to do?*

"What time is it?" Keegan asked, looking for her phone.

"No idea. I fell asleep, too."

"Holy cow." It was after ten. She showed Sammi the phone, and her eyes went wide.

"Okay, well, we definitely napped, didn't we." Her soft laugh brightened the room, and a situation that could've been super awkward seemed to even out. "Sorry about that."

Keegan pushed to her feet—something that was harder than expected, honestly. Her head was light, her ears still felt stuffed with cotton, her mouth was dry, and her entire body ached.

Sammi stood as well and grabbed Keegan's arm to help her balance. "Okay?"

A beat went by, and Keegan nodded. "Yeah."

"How do you feel?"

"Shitty." She sighed, noting that her voice had dropped an octave. "I need to send a text to my boss. There's no way I can teach like this." She fired off a quick text, then turned to Sammi, still standing there like her protector. When she spoke, her voice was quiet. "It was really nice of you, what you did for me."

Sammi shrugged, and Keegan was learning it was a quirk she had when she was feeling exposed—she shrugged like it was no big deal, when they both knew it was. "Well." Sammi cleared her throat. "I didn't want you to be sick all alone." She cleared her throat a second time. "Do you need help getting all set in bed?" She seemed to realize there could be innuendo there, so she rushed into her next sentence without waiting for an answer. "I brought you some NyQuil. It's in the kitchen. Take a dose of that, and you'll sleep like a baby."

"Great. Thank you."

"Okay." Sammi gave one nod, then crossed the room to where she'd left her coat. "There's more soup in the fridge. Don't forget to eat, okay? And if you need anything tomorrow, text me."

"Yes, ma'am." Keegan grinned.

"I mean it."

"It's very cute how you try to be stern." Keegan crossed the room before she could think about it and wrapped her arms around Sammi. "Thank you," she said quietly in her ear.

"Welcome."

She walked her out and stood at the front door of her building until Sammi's car backed out of the parking lot and pulled away, the cold air feeling good on her overheated self as she watched the taillights disappear around the corner. She sucked in a big breath… and then ended up in a coughing fit for several moments before she shut the door and headed back to her apartment.

It didn't take long to find her kitchen to be sparkling clean, the bottle of NyQuil sitting all by itself on the counter like a singer about to give a solo performance. She took a dose, then headed down the short hall to her bedroom.

As she burrowed down into the covers, her head feeling heavy with clogged sinuses, she found herself criticizing her pillow, not nearly as soft and comfy as what she'd been leaning against twenty minutes ago.

With a sad sigh, she closed her eyes.

CHAPTER NINE

It had taken every fiber of her being for Sammi not to drive over to Keegan's the next day and check on her, and if she didn't have a Junebug Farms thing that night, she probably wouldn't have been able to stop herself.

"You are not her girlfriend." She had to say it out loud to herself several times. "She has one, and it's not you. It's Jules." Did she sneer Jules's name? Yeah, a little bit. She couldn't help it, still irritated that Jules chose to protect herself rather than take care of her person when she was sick. As if she needed more reasons not to like the woman.

She had texted a couple times, though. How could she not? Keegan said she was doing okay. Not great, but slightly better than the night before. She'd taken a sick day and would likely take another tomorrow, and she wanted to hear all about how training class went. Sammi promised to update her and even managed not to ask if Jules had shown up yet.

Training class at Junebug took place in a building near the barn on the shelter's grounds. Sammi had never been in that particular one, so she was interested to see it. She'd asked Lisa if it was okay to take Beckett, even though she knew she'd already taken him on a trip and they likely wanted her to showcase other dogs as well. Lisa agreed, maybe seeing how excited Beckett was when he saw Sammi.

"This doesn't suck," Sammi said as Beckett's little nub of a tail wagged his entire back end when he saw her with a leash.

"He's such a great dog," Lisa said, opening the kennel for her. "I wish he had more people looking at him."

"Nobody yet, huh?" Sammi asked, clicking the leash onto his collar.

"Nothing worthwhile. He's intimidating to look at, that's part of the problem. Given the stigma of the pit bull, his chances are slim."

Sammi got down on her knees to receive all the licks and joy from this loving dog. "Yeah, he's so scary," she said, using a horrified voice even as she laughed at his antics. She gave him kisses all over his big square head, and he just wiggled more.

Evan showed up a few minutes later to take some photos in the kennel and then some video following Sammi and Beckett out and along the path to the training facility. The night was cold, their breaths puffs of vapor that floated off into the dark.

"You need a coat, buddy," she said to the dog, but he didn't seem to mind and trotted along happily next to her.

"I think that dog's in love with you," Evan commented as they reached the outbuilding.

"Feeling's mutual," Sammi replied.

Training went great, which was no surprise to Sammi. Beckett was a bit overexcited to be around the other dogs and not separated by a kennel, and she also did notice a couple of the other people keeping an eye on him in their peripheral vision, as if he might spring at them and their dogs. But by the end of class, they seemed to understand he wasn't a threat at all. Just a big hunk of love, all wrapped up in an intimidatingly strong and furry body.

Doing the whole class without Keegan, though, felt strange... which was strange in itself because she did pretty much everything else in her life without Keegan. But the dog stuff, having her photo taken, being videoed, all of it felt wrong without Keegan next to her. She had a great time with Beckett and was shocked by how quickly he learned some things, but she missed Keegan. She owned that.

Once she had said her good-byes and was in her car, she plugged in her phone and hesitated exactly four seconds before dialing Keegan's number, hoping she didn't wake her.

"Hey, you." Keegan's voice was low and hoarse, kind of sexy if Sammi was being honest. "How'd class go?"

"Great. Lisa let me take Beckett again."

Keegan laughed, which then led her to cough. "People are going to think that's the only dog up for adoption."

"I know, right? That's why I asked first. But he's such a sweetheart. He didn't want to go back in his kennel."

"No?"

"I mean, he didn't fight it, but he got noticeably sad. Stopped wagging his tail. Dropped his head. It broke my heart a little bit."

"Sammi. Seriously. Just adopt him. You already love him, and it's clear he loves you."

Sammi sighed. "I know. It's just…a dog is a lot of responsibility, and my hours are long and…"

"I get it. I'm just saying."

"I know." There was a beat of silence. Then, "How are you feeling?"

Keegan gave a little groan. "Like I was run over by a train." She laughed softly. "But better than yesterday, when I felt like I'd been run over by two trains."

"Staying home tomorrow?"

"Yeah, definitely. I want to make sure I'm not contagious before I go back around the kids. Or for Saturday with the carolers."

"Good. Need anything?" She bit the bullet. "Is Jules taking good care of you?"

Was that a snort? A scoff? It was one of those sarcastic sounds. "Jules is staying far, far away so she doesn't *catch the crud*."

Sammi could almost hear the air quotes, and there was so much she wanted to say in that moment. So very much, none of it complimentary to Jules. Instead, she opted for, "I'm sorry, Keegan."

"Eh. What can you do, am I right?"

Sammi knew feigned nonchalance when she heard it, but she didn't push. "All right, well, keep resting, and please, text me if you need anything. Anything. I mean it."

"Yes, ma'am," Keegan said, but her voice was soft, and Sammi could hear the smile in it.

They said their good-byes and hung up, and Sammi pulled out of the parking lot to head home. She sighed.

"Excellent job distancing yourself from her, Sam," she whispered into the dark quiet of the car. "Really excellent. A-plus."

❖

Keegan was completely over her couch. She'd spent most of the day on it, and her back was killing her. She'd headed down the hall to her bedroom around three that afternoon and had been there ever since. Much more comfortable. Closer to the bathroom. More space so the cats wouldn't pin her down—not that it stopped them. The TV was tuned to the ID channel, so she could immerse herself in how horrible some humans actually were. True crime comforted her. She refused to wonder why.

After she hung up with Sammi, she lay there for what felt like a long time. Dusk had come, tugging nighttime by the hand, then leaving it behind. The only light in the room was from the TV, and both cats purred happily, loving having so much time with her.

She picked her phone back up and scrolled to the Junebug Farms Instagram account. Grace was hella fast, and Evan's shots from that night were already up. The post talked about Junebug and the training programs they offered, how they were open to everybody, but if you adopted your dog from them, you got a discount on training. The second paragraph was the same one Grace had been using with each post. It detailed why the shelter was low on funds, what it did for abandoned and rescued animals, and how to donate. Keegan clicked on the photos.

Sammi and Beckett were adorable together. There was no way around it. The dog looked up at her with such love and adoration, it squeezed Keegan's heart a little bit, in the best of ways. It looked like there were a handful of other students there, and Evan had made sure to include them as well. In addition to the photos, there was also a video of Sammi teaching Beckett to stay. It took him a couple of tries—it was clear he wanted to be wherever Sammi was—but on the fourth try, he did it. He stayed where she put him, his entire body vibrating with the clear desire to run to her, and he waited. When she finally gave him the okay, he sprinted across the floor to her like he hadn't seen her in years. It really was a joy to watch.

She replayed it a few more times before finally clicking back over to her text messages. At the top of the list was Sammi, and she'd sent six messages since she'd left last night, all of them short and sweet and just checking to see how she was feeling. Not at all intrusive, but enough to let her know she was being thought of. After Sammi on the list came her mother, then Shannon, then her boss, then the sub who was teaching her class tomorrow, and *then* Jules. Jules, the girl she was supposed to be dating, who hadn't texted her since seven o'clock that morning. When Keegan had been sleeping, by the way.

She dropped her phone on the bed, shaking her head. "What am I doing?" she asked out loud. Bean lifted his head to look at her. "Seriously, Bean, what am I doing? I mean, I get the not wanting to get sick thing, even though I find it a little childish. But one text? All day?" She lifted her hands in a shrug, and let them drop. "What if I'd ended up in the hospital with pneumonia or something? How would she know? She'd have no idea." She stared at the TV but paid no attention to what was on it and shook her head some more. "No. No, you know what? This doesn't work for me."

She knew what she needed to do.

For the next few minutes, she rewatched the video of Sammi and Beckett, and she found herself smiling, not only at Beckett's excitement but also at Sammi's. When she felt her eyes growing heavy, she put a reminder in her phone, then plugged it in and set it on her nightstand. Then she hunkered down into her comforter, leaving the TV on for company. Cocoa adjusted his position so he was curled up near her head, his gentle purring like a white noise machine for her, slowing her heart rate and helping her muscles relax.

She slept better that night than she had in a while, and when she finally woke up, it was because Bean was gently pawing her chin. A glance at her phone told her it was after eight in the morning. The cats usually ate at six thirty, so it was no wonder they wanted her to wake up.

Slowly, she sat up, feeling a bit better than she had yesterday. She was still stuffy, her mouth dry from breathing through it, like she'd been hiking through the desert, but the body aches seemed to be gone. She hadn't had a fever at all yesterday, and today, the headache seemed to be gone as well.

Since she'd already called in sick, she had the day ahead of her, and she vowed that, while she intended to continue to rest because she needed to, she also wasn't going to spend every minute of the day on the couch.

The morning went quickly. She did laundry, washed her sheets and all the blankets she'd wrapped her sick self up in the past couple of days. She ran the vacuum, made herself a smoothie, and took a shower. Once she was clean and smelled good and was back in leggings and a big, comfortable hoodie, she was ready to be back on the couch for a bit. Grabbing her phone, she flopped down and sent a text to Jules.

Hey, could you stop by today? I'd like to talk to you. She didn't send any emoji or let herself dwell too hard on the fact that it was now almost noon and Jules hadn't checked on her once.

The gray dots bounced, then stopped, then bounced, then stopped. Jules was clearly having trouble with a response. Finally, it came. *Oh, babe, I wish I could, but I'm booked solid today.* Then a sad emoji. Oh, wait, then another. And a third. Three sad emoji.

"Ugh, she's gonna make me do this via text," Keegan said out loud with a groan. She sighed as Bean walked onto her lap and bumped his head into her chin. "Okay, okay. I'm on it," she said to him, then typed. She didn't even need to stop and think about her words. They just came out of her fingers and appeared on the screen. *That's what I figured. Listen, this has been fun, but it's not really working for me. Thanks for everything. Take care of yourself.*

She felt lighter. Just like that. As if she'd cut the string that was holding a weight to her, and it dropped to the ground, allowing her to move more freely. The fact that she went the rest of the day without hearing a single other word from Jules told her all she needed to know.

CHAPTER TEN

O h my God, these people are amazing," Sammi whispered, as she leaned in closer to Keegan.

"Right?" Keegan whispered back as "Carol of the Bells" increased in volume. "When do they take a breath?"

Sammi rolled her lips in and bit down on them to keep from laughing.

"Seriously. This song has no pauses. Are they even breathing?" Keegan's eyes were wide. "Someone's gonna drop from lack of oxygen."

They stood off to the side a bit as the Northwood Holiday Choir sang to the residents of Forest Hills Assisted Living, and holy shit, Sammi was entranced. She knew her grandmother went to rehearsals and that she loved being part of the caroling, but her membership was fairly new, and Sammi had never actually heard them perform. They were fabulous. *Fabulous.* They moved smoothly from "Carol of the Bells" into "Silent Night," and Sammi wasn't the only one in awe. The residents that had gathered in the common room to listen were clearly also enraptured, some of them with eyes closed, others who swayed back and forth in their seats. The room lent to the atmosphere, with a fire crackling in the fireplace and a tall Christmas tree in the corner, decorated in white lights and silver garland. A menorah sat on a table by the window. Various candles and decorations were sprinkled around the room.

Sammi and Keegan had brought four dogs this time, two on the larger side and two smaller ones, as Forest Hills had a pretty large population of residents. Evan took photos of them as they all watched, the dogs shockingly well-behaved, at least for the time being, sitting at their feet as the choir sang.

When the performance was over and the applause had died down, an employee from Forest Hills thanked the choir and then told the residents about Junebug Farms and why Sammi and Keegan were there, along with Evan and Grace. Turned out, the majority of the residents were excited to meet the dogs.

Sammi set the terrier mix she'd brought in the lap of one woman who asked politely if she could hold her. "Absolutely. This is Sugar," she said, and the terrier turned in a circle and settled right down on the woman's lap. "Yeah, she clearly hates you." The woman laughed in delight and petted Sugar's head gently. "Can I leave her with you for a minute?"

"You can leave her here all night if you want," the woman said, grinning.

Sammi took the other dog she had with her, a chocolate Lab mix named Chip, and walked around the room with him. He was an old boy but held his head up proudly as people reached out to stroke him. An older man in a wheelchair talked to him.

"Hey, boy. Hi there. How are you?"

Chip seemed to really like him and leaned into his legs.

The man looked up at Sammi. "My Delilah was at Junebug, you know."

"Oh yeah?"

"Can't have pets here, sadly, so I had to give her up."

Sammi's heart squeezed. "Oh no, I'm so sorry."

"No, no. Don't be. She got adopted by a wonderful woman. A teacher. She brings my Delilah by every week to see me."

Sammi pressed a hand to her chest, surprised and grateful the story didn't go in the direction she expected. "She does? Oh wow, that's amazing."

"It really is. Does my heart good to see her and know she's being taken care of."

"I bet it does. That's perfect." As the man doted on Chip,

Sammi gazed around the room. The choir members were chatting with various residents, and the staff had created a little snack area with coffee, Christmas cookies, and eggnog. Keegan was across the room with her two dogs, talking with a couple women. One of them said something funny, and Keegan threw her head back and laughed loudly. Sammi's belly fluttered.

"See something you like, do you?" Her grandmother's voice was quietly teasing behind her, and she turned to meet her smiling gaze.

"You're a barrel of laughs, Grams."

"Just call 'em like I see 'em."

"Also," Sammi said, not purposely trying to change the subject, but happy to, just the same, "you guys are incredible. I had no idea the choir was so good. Wow."

Her grandma's cheeks tinted a soft pink. "Thank you, sweetheart. I'm really enjoying being a part of that group. Nice people. And all ages, which is also nice. I don't feel like I'm stuck in a group of elderly folks."

"Not that there's anything wrong with that," Sammi said with a grin.

"Not that there's anything wrong with that." Her grandma laughed.

The afternoon was lovely, the residents so happy to give the dogs some love. They also shared their Christmas cookies, which four of the residents had baked themselves, and holy deliciousness, they were good.

She and Keegan bade good-bye to Grams, who was going to hang out for just a bit longer, since some of the choir members wanted to sing another song or two, and loaded up the van.

On the ride back to Junebug, all five of them talked about the visit.

"That choir," Trent said from the driver's seat. "Good God."

"Right?" Grace agreed. "They were unbelievable."

"I think I ate my weight in Christmas cookies," Sammi said with a grimace, and Keegan laughed.

"How could you not? They were so good." There was a beat, then Keegan said, "Hey, Trent, I have a question."

"Shoot."

"Why is Junebug sending us with dogs to places that can't have dogs?"

Trent opened his mouth to answer at the same time Grace held up her hand and rubbed her fingers and thumb together. He nodded. "Exactly. We hope they might donate. You'd be surprised the level of donations we get from the elderly community."

Keegan nodded. "I see. I had no idea."

"Well, that was a fun afternoon. And only one accident." Sammi glanced over her shoulder at the crates in the back. "It's okay, Sugar. We all get a little excited sometimes."

Junebug wasn't terribly busy when they got back, which was surprising for a Saturday, but then Sammi heard the woman behind the desk telling Grace that it had been a zoo earlier. That was great news.

They took the dogs back to the dog wing. Lisa had gone home for the night, but there was another woman there who smiled and helped them put the dogs back into their kennels. Sammi, of course, stopped to give Beckett some love. While he was clearly happy to see her, he was also much more low key than he usually was, and it squeezed Sammi's heart.

She and Keegan left the dog wing together. In the lobby, Sammi put a hand on Keegan's arm. "Hey, what are you doing for dinner?"

Keegan leaned an elbow on the front desk as she said, "Well, I was planning on a very exciting evening of frozen mac and cheese and a true crime documentary. Why?"

"My grandma's making her famous veggie lasagna for dinner. Wanna join?"

"You know what? That sounds better than dinner alone. I'd love to."

"Great!"

Keegan pulled out her phone and held it up. "I need to make a quick call. Can I meet you there? What time?"

Sammi nodded. "Absolutely. Come as soon as you're done. Just park across the street in my driveway. You know which house is my grandma's?" Keegan nodded, and Sammi rapped her knuckles on the desk. "Awesome. See you shortly." She pointed at Keegan as she backed toward the door. "Drive carefully."

Once outside, she exhaled in relief. She had no idea where that invitation had come from or how she'd managed to extend it without making a fool of herself, but she'd done it. She started her car and got out to brush off the thin dusting of snow that had covered it since they'd been gone. Then she zipped one row back and cleared off Keegan's, too. Back in her own car, she plugged in her phone, put the car in gear, and told Siri to call her grandmother. When she answered, Sammi couldn't keep the smile from her face.

"Hey, Grams. You home? Done dazzling the residents of Forest Hills?"

"Just got here, yup."

"I'm bringing company for dinner. That's okay, right?"

❖

"Are you sure this is a good idea?" Sammi's mom's brow was furrowed with concern.

"What do you mean?" Sammi was helping her set the table for four, laying out forks and the fancy dishes Grandma always used on weekends.

"You know exactly what I mean, Samantha." Her mom's voice wasn't exactly stern, but it was definitely serious. "You like this girl as more than a friend. She's hurt you once, and now she has a girlfriend. What are you doing?"

Sammi tightened her jaw, not wanting to snap at her mom and also not wanting to respond to that statement at all. That very, very accurate statement. She also didn't want to answer the question, because the answer to the question was that she had no freaking idea. What was she doing? Not a clue. All she did know was that any chance she got where she could spend time with Keegan, she was probably going to jump at. Bad decision or not.

Her grandmother came out of the kitchen then, oven mitts on her hands, a huge, bubbling pan of lasagna between them.

"Oh my God, that smells amazing," Sammi said, just as the doorbell rang. "Got it." She hurried to the door and, hand on the knob, she took a deep breath in through her nose and let it out slowly. Then she pulled it open.

She'd seen Keegan hundreds of times over the course of their friendship, so how was it that she always felt like she was seeing her for the first time? Her auburn hair was down, and it had started to snow out, so flakes were melting on it. She wore a black wool peacoat and boots and carried a bottle of wine in her gloved hands.

"Hi," she said, and her blue eyes danced. "Long time, no see."

"Right?" Sammi said and stepped aside. "Come in. Starting to snow, I see."

"Just a little." Keegan came in and handed the bottle to Sammi while she toed off her boots and unbuttoned her coat.

Sammi hung it up for her, handed her back the wine, and said, "Come in. You're right on time."

"God, it smells incredible in here," Keegan said as they rounded the corner into the dining room.

Greetings went all around, and her grandma gave Keegan a big hug. "Nice to see you again."

"Thank you so much for having me." Keegan handed over the wine. "The girl at the wine store said this would pair well with lasagna, so I hope she was right."

Before long, they were all seated at the table and enjoying dinner together.

"Oh my God," Keegan said, through a mouthful of lasagna. "This is *so good*."

Sammi's grandma beamed. "Aren't you sweet."

"No, seriously. This is fantastic." She scooped another forkful into her mouth.

What was wrong with Sammi? There had to be something because she was enjoying watching Keegan eat way too much. *Way* too much. She glanced up and caught her mother's eye, one eyebrow arched in disapproval.

"So, Keegan, are you from here in Northwood?" her mother asked.

Keegan nodded as she chewed her mouthful of food. "Yup. Born and raised. I love it here."

"Yeah? Me, too. What's your favorite place downtown?" Her mother was all about the questions tonight.

"Oh, that's easy. The gazebo in McInerny Park."

Sammi's head whipped around. "Seriously? I love that place."

"Right?" Keegan said. "It's the best place to just sit and hang, especially in the evening when it's dark and the park is empty."

"So peaceful," Sammi agreed. A beat went by before the subject was changed.

"How did things go today?" her grandma asked, thank God. "I was busy singing and then chatting with the choir. How did the dogs do?"

"I'd say they were hits," Sammi said. "Except for when Sugar peed on the floor."

"There was a lot going on," her grandmother said. "I'm sure the poor thing was nervous."

"Your choir was amazing, Mrs. Sorenson. Like, astonishingly good," Keegan said. "Right?" She turned to Sammi.

A nod. "They were incredible. I can't believe I've never heard you sing with them before. And the residents were so nice. Oh! I forgot to tell you, one of the men there said he had to give his dog up when he moved into Forest Hills, but that a teacher adopted her and brings her to visit him all the time."

"That's so sweet," Keegan said.

"I wondered if you knew the teacher, but I forgot to ask what her name was." She frowned.

"I mean, I do know every teacher at every school in Northwood," Keegan said, a teasing lilt in her tone.

"Valid," Sammi said with a laugh.

Her grandmother stood up to refill wineglasses all around. When she got to Keegan, she asked, "So, how's…I'm sorry, what was her name again? Julia?"

"Jules," Keegan said, holding her glass out. "She's gone." It was a simple statement, very matter-of-fact. Then, "Whoa, whoa, whoa," as Sammi's grandma nearly overflowed Keegan's glass.

"She's gotta drive, Grams," Sammi said, not sure what to do with the weird nervous feeling suddenly rolling around in her stomach.

"Sorry about that," her grandma said with a laugh. She returned to her own seat, picked up her fork, and asked, "Gone as in...out of town?"

Sammi looked down at her plate and closed her eyes, and much as she wanted to send an irritated glare across the table at her grandmother, she also wanted to hear the answer.

"Oh no. Gone from my life. It wasn't working out." Keegan didn't seem embarrassed or sad or, honestly, any emotion at all around this news, and Sammi had to try hard to contain her happiness.

"That's too bad," Sammi's mother said. "Breakups are hard. I'm sorry."

Keegan shook her head. "Don't be. We hadn't dated long." She laughed softly. "Trust me, I'm not heartbroken about it."

Sammi raised her glass. "To not being heartbroken."

"Hear, hear," her grandma said, and they all clinked glasses in the center of the table.

"So, what's next on the shelter dog project?" Sammi's mother asked, finally wading into the conversation.

Sammi and Keegan looked at each other blankly for a beat. Two. Then they both burst out laughing. "I have no idea," Keegan said.

Sammi held up a finger. "Hang on." She pulled out her phone and scrolled to her email to find the schedule. "Oh, crap, it's tomorrow."

"It is? What are we doing?"

Sammi set the phone down and looked at Keegan with a huge grin. "Apparently, we're sledding."

❖

The sled gods were smiling on all the kids who hoped to go sledding on Sunday. Barker's Creek Park—aptly named for any dog-related activities—had an enormous hill that was hugely popular for sledding, and it had been snowing for several hours by the time Keegan woke up Sunday morning.

She gazed out her kitchen window as she sipped her morning coffee. They'd accumulated several inches overnight, and the snow was still falling in big, fat, fluffy flakes. Her check of her weather app said it was twenty-nine degrees headed to a high of thirty-five, kind of perfect for sledding.

She planned to walk to Barker's Creek Park. It was literally ten minutes from her apartment building. She'd talked to Sammi about it last night, and Sammi was going to walk as well, though it would be a longer trek for her. Trent would meet them there with Grace, Evan, and whatever dogs had been chosen for this event.

Thinking of Sammi made her mind drift back to last night and that fabulous, strange, momentarily awkward but mostly awesome dinner with Sammi and her family. Mia had definitely been fishing for information, that was obvious. And Sammi was mortified by it, which was also obvious, and Keegan was glad about that because it hopefully meant that Sammi hadn't put her grandmother up to it. All that being said, though, Keegan found herself surprisingly relieved to have the news about Jules's departure from her life out on the table.

Jules hadn't even tried to convince her otherwise, which really said all she needed to know, didn't it?

"Good riddance," she whispered as she searched her closet for something to wear. Cocoa was lounging on the bed, watching her as if ready to render an opinion. She couldn't remember the last time she went sledding—had she still been a teenager?—so she did her best to dress in layers. Thermal underwear, bottoms and top, wool socks, fleece-lined pants, and a sweatshirt. Then at the front door, she added a ski jacket, boots, a knit hat, and some mittens that she hoped were waterproof. Once the temperature climbed above freezing, the snow would become wetter.

She bid her cats good-bye and headed toward the park. The

air was brisk, but not freezing cold. While playing in the snow wouldn't be her first choice of a weekend activity in December, she was feeling the tiniest bit excited about it.

By the time she got to the hill, the snow had stopped, and the clouds were moving out so peeks of sunshine could stream in. Trent had already arrived. She could see the Junebug Farms van parked among the other cars. She could also see dozens of kids and parents and sleds. The place was hopping, that was for sure. It brought a smile to her face.

Grace saw her first. "Hey there," she said as she held out an arm toward the hill. "What a day for this, huh?"

"It's gorgeous. I can't believe the sun's coming out. I thought it was gonna snow all day." She peeked into the van to see two very furry dogs in crates, waiting to come out and play. "Hi, guys," she said to them, and the one that looked to be some kind of Aussie mix began to wag its butt, as its tail was just a little nub. The other one watched her with its one blue eye and one brown eye, its pointy ears and gray coloring telling her it might have some husky in it.

"This is Sheba," Trent said of the husky, then pointed at the Aussie. "And this is Marco."

"Are you guys ready to play in the snow? Yeah?" She gave them each pets, and Trent got them out and leashed up.

Keegan checked her phone several times, wondering where Sammi was, but finally saw her cresting the hill to her left. The way her heart picked up speed? Yeah, she tried hard not to notice. She failed. "You made it," she said as Sammi got closer.

"I did." Slightly out of breath, Sammi inhaled deeply. "Longer walk than I expected. Hi."

Sammi looked super cute in her winter gear. Her ski jacket was red and black, and her black knit hat matched her black mittens. It was a sleek look, but also playful. It suited her well. Her cheeks were rosy from her walk, and her eyes were bright.

Trent came up to them with a leash in each hand and a dog at the end of each leash. Both dogs wore deep green vests with gold letters that read ADOPT ME. "Ladies, your playmates for the day." Grace and Evan joined him.

"So," Grace said, "I think what we'll do is have you both wander around the park with the dogs first. Just get people seeing them, especially the kids. We'll get some stills and some video. Then, if you guys want to sled, we can get some of that as well."

"Sounds good," Keegan said, taking Sheba's leash. Sammi took Marco, and they headed down the side of the hill so they could walk around the park a bit and let the dogs sniff.

It was fun to watch Sammi interact with the kids who came up to her and Marco. Sheba was a bit intimidating, and maybe a bit intimidated, so they stood off to the side a bit and let folks come up to them if they wanted to pet her. But Marco was all about the kids. His entire back end wagged nonstop whenever he got any attention, and Sammi was just as cute. She squatted down to be eye level with the littler kids. She remained slightly aloof around the older kids, who were clearly sucked in by the mystery woman with the cool dog.

The sun was great, and the sky was a breathtaking blue, but it didn't warm up much, and after an hour, Keegan's fingertips were nearly numb. Sheba didn't seem bothered at all and, at one point, lay right down in the snow to watch the people sledding.

"Hey," Grace said as she came up behind her. "How do you guys feel about taking a run or two down the hill. Without the dogs," she added with a grin.

What she really wanted was to go home, make some hot cocoa, and pile on the couch in her sweats. But she nodded instead and indicated Sammi several yards away. "I'm in if she's in."

She watched as Grace crossed to where Sammi and Marco were chatting with a young boy and his parents. Adoption potential, maybe? She crossed her very cold fingers inside her mittens as she watched Sammi nod, then turn and look her way with a big smile.

Not long after that, the dogs were back in their crates in the warm van, and Keegan sat her butt on a blue plastic toboggan.

"Perfect," Evan was saying. "The sled and the sky are almost exactly the same color. I love it. Okay, Sammi, you sit here. Spread your legs, Keegan."

Did her face turn red? Because she felt it heat up at the double entendre of his words and hoped nobody else noticed. Though if Sammi's not-very-hidden grin was any indication, she *had* noticed. She plopped herself in front of Keegan and tucked her legs onto the plastic as best she could. It was tight, her back pressed all up against Keegan's front. Despite the cold, she could still smell the raspberry scent of Sammi's hair where it peeked out from under her hat.

"Bring your legs in," Sammi said, yanking Keegan out of her daydream.

"What?"

Sammi patted her thighs with her mittened hands. "These. Bring 'em in or you're gonna wreck us."

"Oh! Oh, right." And she moved her legs so they were inside the toboggan, and pressed up against Sammi's, and Keegan realized in that moment that pretty much every part of their bodies were touching. Legs, torsos, arms, even their heads were close enough to press together.

Sammi grabbed both Keegan's hands and wrapped them around her torso. "Hold on to me. I don't want to go flying off."

Keegan tightened her grip.

"Ready?" Grace asked as Evan was snapping away.

"Hang on," he said, then hurried about halfway down the hill. When he seemed to find a spot he liked, he waved back to Grace.

Sammi patted her on the leg. "Ready?"

"Ready," Keegan said, then felt Grace's hands on her back. "Go!"

They slid over the crest of the hill and tipped down, picking up speed alarmingly fast. The snow had been packed solid from everybody sledding on it all day, and now it was almost ice. The toboggan shot downward, past Evan, who had his phone up, taking great video, she hoped. A whoop of delight came from Sammi, who threw her arms up in the air as if they were on a roller coaster as she leaned back into Keegan.

She tightened her grip on Sammi until the hill leveled off and they began to slow, finally cruising to a stop. Sammi still lay against her, breathing heavily, her breaths puffs of vapor in the cold air, a huge smile on her face.

"That was *amazing*."

"That was terrifying," Keegan said with a laugh.

Sammi turned so she could see her face. "It was? Does that mean you won't do it one more time?" Her expression was...sad wasn't the right word. Concerned? Hopeful? Both things? Sammi wanted to do another run, that was clear. And what Keegan wanted was to make her happy.

Without stopping to examine that, she said simply, "I can do one more run."

"Yes!" Sammi moved her arm in a fist pump, then turned and planted a loud, smacking kiss on Keegan's cheek. "Come on, let's go!"

Keegan was hauled to her feet, and they began the trek back up the hill. She couldn't help the smile on her face.

❖

"You doing okay?" Keegan asked Sammi as they walked.

"I'm fucking freezing," Sammi replied with a laugh. "That last wipeout got me good."

Keegan chuckled along with her. "You *had* to do one more run."

"I did." Sammi shook her head with a smile as she recalled insisting on one last run down the hill. Keegan had bowed out, so Sammi went alone. On her stomach. She had to zig and zag to avoid a couple of kids and ended up tipping herself right out of the toboggan toward the bottom of the hill where the snow was no longer smooth and icy.

"I pretty much filled my jacket with snow," she said with an exaggerated shiver.

"I know. I was there." Keegan laughed softly again. "We're almost home. Hang in there."

Ten minutes later, they were in Keegan's apartment, and then she was in Keegan's bedroom with some of Keegan's sweats, Keegan ordering her out of her clothes so she could toss them in the dryer.

"I'll get changed and make us some hot chocolate."

What a day, Sammi thought, replaying all their fun in her head. The dogs, the sledding, the shots Evan had captured. Several people had stopped them to ask for details about both Marco and Sheba, and she was pretty sure they'd both be adopted by Christmas. Trent said several more folks stopped by the van to get information about donating. It was a successful day, she'd say. And now, she was standing in Keegan's bedroom about to put on some of her clothes.

She took a moment to look around. Being in somebody's bedroom was a privilege, as it was often a sanctuary. The walls were white—as was the whole apartment because Keegan rented, she didn't own—but there was lots of sunny yellow to brighten things up. Her bed was a queen, her comforter white with a bright yellow abstract design. Lots of pillows. In fact, it was so inviting, Sammi had to make a conscious effort not to dive onto it and burrow into those pillows. She had one large dresser, the surface very clean except for a small jewelry box and two framed photos. One was of three people that must have been her family—two older folks who were likely Keegan's parents, and Shannon, who was so much a younger version of Keegan. The other was of her cats, lounging in a ray of sunlight. There was a small desk tucked in a corner, also very neat. The nightstands held matching lamps, and a stack of books and a glass of water rested on one.

Keegan sleeps on the left, Sammi thought with a smile. Shaking herself into action, she stripped out of her very wet clothes and stepped into Keegan's. The sweatpants were gray and a tiny bit long on her, and the hoodie was navy blue and very worn in, super soft. Everything smelled clean and fresh and like Keegan, and Sammi took a moment to stand there with her head inside the sweatshirt and just inhale.

All right. Pull yourself together.

She gathered her things and headed out to the kitchen. "Hi," she said, as Keegan pulled mugs from a cabinet. "Where's the dryer?"

Keegan had taken clothes with her when she left Sammi in her room and now looked as comfortable as Sammi felt in black joggers and an oversized red sweatshirt, the neckline worn and ragged.

Keegan turned to look at her, then blinked several times and had to clear her throat. "Oh, right here. Gimme." She took Sammi's wet clothes from her hands and opened a discreet folding door in the hall that hid a stacking washer and dryer.

"Oh, sneaky."

"It was a requirement in an apartment for me. I love my mom, but I was not about to schlep my laundry to her house every weekend like a college kid. And Laundromats skeeve me out."

Sammi laughed. "Understood."

Back in the kitchen, the water was boiling, so Keegan poured it into the mugs with the hot chocolate, and then handed one to Sammi. She pulled out whipped cream and marshmallows and spoons.

"Wow. You have all the trimmings," Sammi commented with an approving nod, picking up her spoon to stir.

"My mom always put either whipped cream or marshmallows in my hot chocolate when I was a kid, and now it feels naked without them."

"Naked hot chocolate. Interesting." *Oh yes, keep hitting her with random sexual innuendos. That's not awkward at all.* Sammi sighed internally, annoyed at herself. She reached for the marshmallows and stuffed three into her mug.

"You don't mess around."

"Not when it comes to marshmallows. No."

"Wanna sit?"

They moved to the living room and sat on the couch at opposite ends. There was a cat on the back of the couch, and another lying in front of the heat vent down by the floor. Sammi watched as Keegan sat, legs folded under her, so she was facing Sammi, mug in hand. "I thought today went well."

Sammi nodded. "Me, too. Lots of questions from lots of people."

"I wonder if Jessica is happy with the way things have gone. Do you think we're raising money?"

"It's kind of hard to tell, isn't it?" Sammi ventured a sip of her hot chocolate, the marshmallows buffering her lips from the too hot liquid. "I bet my grandma would know."

"You mean your grandma the matchmaker?" Keegan's voice held a hint of playfulness, but Sammi still felt herself blanch.

"Oh God, I'm so sorry about that. She thinks she's being subtle when she's really not." Ugh. She'd suspected Keegan knew exactly what her grandma was doing, but to have her say it out loud was just mortifying.

But Keegan laughed softly and waved a dismissive hand and didn't seem upset by it at all. "Don't be. I think it's cute." Then she sipped her hot chocolate, and her eyes stayed on Sammi over the rim the whole time. She had a trace of marshmallow on her top lip, which she swiped off with her tongue, and everything in Sammi headed south. "She really wants us together," Keegan said softly, and the tone of her voice seemed almost amused.

Sammi struggled for words for a beat before saying again, "Sorry about that." What else could she say?

Again, Keegan smiled and didn't seem to be bothered at all. "I think it's sweet."

"You do?"

Keegan nodded and sipped again. Then she completely changed the subject. "So. Only ten days until Christmas. What do we have left in our queenly duties?"

Sammi didn't have to look at her phone. She'd checked earlier. "Just two things left." She'd been both relieved and disappointed when she'd seen that. "We're bringing gifts to the kids in the pediatric unit of the hospital who have to stay there over Christmas. Next Saturday. The parade is at eleven, then we go to the hospital."

"Oh, the kids will be so happy to see the dogs."

"I think Jessica is getting a couple of them cleared to be there." She frowned. "I think it'll be a mixed bag. It's so sad that they have to be there over Christmas."

Keegan leaned forward and patted her knee. "We'll cheer them up. That'll be our job. Presents and dogs. What's not to love? You should bring Beckett."

"I'm not sure he's one who's getting cleared, but maybe."

"Fingers crossed."

They were quiet for a moment, each lost in their own thoughts about kids in hospitals over Christmas. When Sammi pulled herself out of her own head, Keegan was looking at her, head tipped to the side. "What?"

"I like you here in my space."

Well, that was a surprise. "Yeah?"

"Mm-hmm."

"I like being in your space."

Their gazes held. "What if I pop some popcorn and refill our hot chocolate and we curl up under a blanket and watch a Christmas movie?" Keegan grimaced. "Does that sound boring?"

"Are you kidding? That sounds absolutely perfect." And it did.

It didn't take long with them working together. Keegan popped a big bowl of popcorn, complete with melted butter, while Sammi refilled their mugs. Her clothes had dried, so she removed them from the dryer and folded them into a neat pile, then laid them on a chair by the door, in no hurry to give up wearing Keegan's clothes. Soon they were back in the living room.

Keegan pulled a big, fluffy green blanket off the back of the couch, then sat down in the middle and patted the spot next to her. "Sit, so we both have blanket."

Sammi swallowed but did as she was told, and soon she was warm and toasty, covered in the soft blanket, her thigh pressed against Keegan's, a bowl of popcorn balanced directly between them. Keegan put her feet up on the coffee table and crossed her legs at the ankle, so Sammi did the same. It was blissful comfort, and she never wanted to move.

"What should we watch?" Keegan asked.

"I don't care," Sammi said, and it was the most honest thing she'd said all day. Keegan could put on WWE wrestling or a monster truck rally, and she'd be fine with that, as long as she could stay right where she was until the end of time.

"Understood," Keegan said, and it seemed like she actually did. She pushed buttons on the remote until a Hallmark movie popped up.

It was perfect. If Sammi had to describe a more perfect winter afternoon, she wouldn't have been able to. The movie, the popcorn, the company. Especially the company. She didn't really pay attention to the movie. She didn't have to. Somebody returned to their tiny hometown from the big city, fell in love with the person they dated in high school, and decided not to go back to the big city. Sure, there were some other details thrown in there—a factory being shut down or a Christmas concert in danger of being canceled or something like that—but the ending was the same as every other movie like it. A happily ever after, usually complete with either softly falling snow or a giant Christmas tree lighting in the center of town. Sammi didn't care. She loved every one of those movies, some more than others, but every one of them, and it made for the most blissful setting of the evening.

As if reading her mind, Keegan gave a soft, dreamy sigh. "I know people mock these movies, but I don't care. They serve a purpose. They make me happy. And they make me excited about Christmas."

"Hundred percent," Sammi said, and when she turned to look at Keegan, she realized just how close their faces were. They'd hunkered down under the blanket. Their thighs touched. Their shoulders touched. And their faces were so close. Very close. Dangerously close. Too close. All she needed to do was lean the tiniest bit, and their lips would meet. Just the slightest lean—

And then Keegan leaned.

Their lips met.

It was soft. Tender. Sweet.

"Oh," Keegan said as they parted, and she brought her fingertips to her lips. She appeared more surprised than horrified. "I'm so sorry," she whispered.

"I'm not," Sammi said. A soft smile later, she slid out from under the blanket. "I think I should probably go." She moved to the chair where her clothes were piled, then toward the door where her boots and coat were.

"Okay," Keegan said quietly.

"You sure?" Sammi asked. Keegan blinked at her, and words seemed to escape her. "Oh, you're not sure. Good. That's good." She quickly ordered an Uber on her phone, then stepped into her boots and slipped on her coat. The whole time, Keegan stayed on the couch, blinking and looking a little bit confused.

Sammi was okay with that.

Finally, as she was zipping up her coat, Keegan pushed to her feet and walked toward her. She cleared her throat before saying, "I'm really glad you came."

"You know what, Keegan? This was the best day I've had in a really long time. Thank you for that." She reached out and gave her a quick hug, forced herself not to linger, not to inhale deeply and take in Keegan's scent, not to tighten her hold and wish to hold her forever. Just a quick hug, and then she let go. "I'll get these clothes back to you soon." As if on cue, her phone notified her of the arrival of her Uber. She held it up and tipped it back and forth as proof. "Talk to you later, yeah?"

Without waiting for a response, she pushed out the door and hurried down to the lobby, smiling. She didn't look back. Leaving Keegan with her clearly complicated feelings was the absolute right move. She was sure of it.

CHAPTER ELEVEN

Thank fucking God it was the last day of school before the holiday break. Thank. Fucking. God.

It was all Keegan could think about. Well. *Almost* all. It was Friday the twentieth. Just one weekend and two weekdays until Christmas. Thank fucking God.

The kids had lost their minds. She couldn't help but smile and shake her head as her students ran around the room, playing loudly, shouting, singing. None of it was negatively rambunctious. They were just super excited. Of course they were. They were kids, and they were about to have two solid weeks off from school. What was there *not* to be excited about?

What a weird, weird week.

She'd spent the past five days stuck in her own head about what had happened on Sunday. It had been the most perfect day—Sammi had been right about that, without question. And then they'd kissed.

And then they'd kissed.

It wasn't hot and heavy, like the last time they'd kissed. It wasn't urgent or frantic or heated, like the last time they'd kissed. Not at all. Not even a little. It had been…gentle. Thoughtful. Sentimental, even. And it had left her thinking about it for nearly a week, her head spinning. What the hell?

They hadn't talked about it. She'd wanted to bring it up, but had chickened out each time she had the chance. Sammi had been her usual fun, casual self in their texts and hadn't said a thing about it either, though if it was because she was as freaked as Keegan was or because it didn't matter to her, she wasn't sure.

She took a seat at her desk, propped her elbows on it, and dug all her fingers into her hair. She wanted to groan out loud but didn't want to weird out her kids—not that they'd notice, the way they were running all over the place. A glance at the big clock on the wall told her she only needed to hang on for a few more minutes.

Somehow, she managed to.

Later that night, her sister was giving her the look.

"Okay, what's going on with you?" Shannon asked as they sat at the island in their mom's kitchen drinking wine. It was tradition on the last day of school before any significant breaks. Keegan went to her parents' house and had a drink with her mom to celebrate. Shannon had been joining in since she got back from college.

"What do you mean, what's going on?" Keegan did her best to come across as indignant at such an assumption.

"No, she's right," their mom said. "Something's up with you." She laid a piece of cheese on a cracker and pointed to Keegan before popping it in her mouth. "Talk."

Keegan blinked rapidly and looked from one of them to the other, all prepared for denial. Then she sighed and dropped the act. They knew her too well. "Sammi kissed me." The silence was deafening as Shannon and their mom exchanged a glance. Keegan squinted at them. "What?"

"Sammi has kissed you before. Why is this news?" Shannon asked.

Keegan sighed. "Yes, Shannon, I know that. I'm saying she did it again. After a year. But this was…different somehow." God, she didn't want to get into all of it with her family. All the ins and outs and strangeness and how she was just a weirdo who was clearly a mess about so many things and—

"Honey." Her mom waited until she met her gaze. "Talk to us. What's going on?"

Another big sigh, because that's all she could seem to manage. "I honestly don't know. Last year, I just…It was all so big. So much.

I felt…" She moved her hands in front of her chest in an attempt to put some kind of words to what she'd been feeling then, but she trailed off, took a big sip of her wine, and tried to find the right explanation. "It was so big, it overwhelmed me. And I got scared."

"Don't you think—and hear me out," her mother said. "You should maybe talk to her?"

"God, that's your solution to everything, isn't it? Open communication. Geez, Mom, sing a new song," Keegan said, then laughed. "I know. I know. You're right. I just…I didn't expect that she'd still be interested, and then this Christmas queens thing happened…"

"Rigged," Shannon said, slicing some cheese.

Keegan laughed softly. "I just didn't expect all of this. Whatever it is."

"Yeah." Her mom reached for the wine bottle and refilled all their glasses. "But you could do so much worse than Dr. Sorenson, you know."

"Even I think she's hot," Shannon chimed in. "And I'm all about the dick."

Keegan barked out a laugh as their mother smacked at her youngest. "Shannon Marie!"

Their laughter died down, and her mother reached over to grasp Keegan's forearm. "I hate seeing you so discombobulated."

"Impressive word, Mom." Keegan grinned.

"Keegan. I'm serious."

"I know."

"Talk to her."

Keegan looked from her mother to her sister, who nodded her agreement, took a deep breath, and let it out. "Okay. I will."

❖

Keegan had kissed her.

That was the thought that ran through Sammi's mind for nearly an entire week solid, and she still couldn't get over it. *Keegan* had kissed her. *Keegan* had made the move. It was so unexpected, and when Sammi thought back, when she replayed the whole thing in her mind, she was so proud of herself. For how calm she'd stayed. For how she'd managed to get up and head home without taking Keegan's face in both hands and kissing her senseless, which was what she'd *really* wanted to do.

But that's what had happened last time, and it had been a disaster, and she wasn't risking doing that again. No way.

"Yes, yes, I'm very proud of you," Chrissy said when they FaceTimed Friday night, but there was a slight edge in her voice, like she was irritated with Sammi. "But I'm also worried about you."

Sammi snorted and waved a dismissive hand.

Chrissy pointed at her through the screen. "No. Don't you do that. I was there the last time Hurricane Keegan happened, remember? You were heartbroken."

Sammi sighed because Chrissy wasn't wrong. "I know. I know. But..." She sighed again. "Maybe I'm just being ridiculous."

"And that's different than any other day...how?"

"Hilarious. You're hilarious. You should take that on the road. Open for Taylor Tomlinson. Do a Netflix special."

"Maybe I will," Chrissy said, feigning indignation. "But I'm serious, Sam. Please be careful."

"I will. I promise. There are only two things left anyway."

"Which are?"

"The parade is first. We'll ride on the Junebug float. Then we take the dogs to visit the kids who will be in the hospital over the holidays."

"Oh no, that makes me so sad."

"Hopefully, we'll give them a bit of cheer."

"And what happens after these two events? You're just done?"

"Yup." She injected as much nonchalance into her voice as possible because the reality was, she had no idea what to do after tomorrow. Chase Keegan? Again? Risk what happened last time? Because in truth, she didn't actually know what had happened last time, did she?

They chatted a bit more, then Chrissy had to go and they hung up, but the cheer and sliver of happiness that had been hanging out with her all week began to wane a bit. Leave it to her BFF to hit her with the reality stick. Or the reality two-by-four, in this case.

She was a bit lower-key for the rest of the evening. She made herself some pancakes, because breakfast for dinner was the best thing in the world. She watched a movie she'd been wanting to see. Then she took a book up to her bedroom. But the whole time, she felt like she was acting. Like she was going through the motions of what a person does in the evening, how a regular person spends their Friday night if they're not going out. But in the back of her mind, there was a little stress. There were questions. There was wonder and confusion and hope and not a small amount of irritation.

Falling asleep that night was hard.

❖

The next morning was Saturday, and it brought a bit more clarity.

Sammi lay in bed, the sun beaming low through her slightly open blinds, telling her it was later than her usual wake-up time. She'd stayed up too late reading and had slept fitfully, so it didn't surprise her when she glanced at her phone to see it was after eight. But she felt better, much better than she had after her call with Chrissy, because she understood now that she simply needed to talk to Keegan even though a year ago they'd agreed never to discuss that night again. Wasn't it interesting when a solution was that clear, but people didn't see it? She'd been reading a romance novel and the entire conflict between the leads was caused by them not having a conversation they should've absolutely had.

Don't be as dumb as these fictional characters was the thought that had lulled her to sleep.

So, she would not, she'd decided.

❖

The Christmas parade float for Junebug Farms wasn't complicated. It couldn't really be because dogs were going to be riding on it, and any kind of fancy mechanical noisemakers or whirring things would likely frighten them. Therefore, it was a pretty simple pickup truck, decorated with lots of twinkle lights, Rudolph antlers on either side window, a big red nose on the front grille, and a lit Christmas tree in the bed. A banner on each side of the truck announced it was the Junebug Farms float, featuring their Christmas queens, and a big speaker was fastened to the roof, piping holiday tunes into the air as they crawled along the parade route. There were cozy blankets around the tree where Sammi, Keegan, and three dogs sat, and despite the chill in the air, Keegan felt warm and comfortable.

"This is pretty amazing," Sammi said, leaning close so she could be heard over the music, as well as the cheering of the crowd.

Keegan liked her being this close, she couldn't lie about that. Part of the reason she wasn't cold was because Sammi's warm body was so close. The other part, of course, was the twenty pounds of dog in her lap and the chin and head of another that was splayed across her shin. "It really is," she said, raising her voice.

And it was. Keegan had never been in a parade before. Oh sure, she'd sat on the side of the street and watched many of them in her life, but not once had she ever marched or ridden or participated in any way. This was all new to her, and she kind of loved waving to the crowd, seeing how much love there was for the dogs, the other animals, and Junebug Farms in general. More than once, somebody in the crowd held up a rainbow flag, cheering for the two queens of Junebug Farms. The parade route happened to pass by a local gay bar, and the roar and cheers that came from it as they rolled slowly by made Keegan so proud.

"Oh my God," Sammi said, as she waved to the LGBTQ crowd that had formed in front of the bar. "Look at them all." The Lab mix with her barked at the people happily, as if they were cheering just for him.

"It's incredible!" Keegan shouted happily, her pride in who she was surging higher than it had in a long time. She turned her gaze to

Sammi and grinned at her. "I'm so happy to be here right now with you."

"Yeah?"

"Absolutely."

Sammi's smile grew wide, and her eyes sparkled with unmistakable joy. Keegan loved knowing she'd put that look on Sammi's face, that she'd been the one to make her so happy in that moment. She reached for Sammi's gloved hand with her own mittened one and squeezed it.

It couldn't have been more perfect. The weather was inarguably wintery, with a dull gray sky and light flurries in the air, but the temperature wasn't horrible, and most people watching the procession seemed comfortable and happy. Keegan had brought an insulated container of hot chocolate for each of them, and now she sipped happily, the warm sweetness spreading from her stomach outward. She had a bag of dog treats from Makenna Covington's shop, and she gave each dog a bite every so often to keep them occupied.

I don't want this to end.

It was a thought that ran through her head for the entire length of the parade, surprising her at first, but then settling into her soul and making itself at home. She tossed a glance at Sammi, who was waving in the other direction but then turned to catch Keegan's eye and pointed. "The gang from my practice," she said, her eyes bright with excitement, her cheeks flushed a pretty pink from the cold. Keegan scooted closer—trying not to disturb the little guy in her lap too much—so she was looking over Sammi's shoulder as a handful of women jumped up and down cheering for them. She waved back and inadvertently inhaled the scent of Sammi, warm and inviting.

When she sat back down, it was a little bit closer to Sammi than before.

The whole parade went like that—waving and cheering and petting dogs and trying to get closer to Sammi. And much as she'd wanted it to last forever, it did have to come to an end. The parade finished at a Christmas festival in the park. Junebug Farms had a booth where folks could donate, get information on adoptions, and meet the dogs from the float, which Keegan and Sammi handed off. Reluctantly.

Keegan squatted down and took the face of the little dog who'd served as her blanket for the entire parade in both her hands. "You are such a good boy. You're gonna make some family really lucky." Then she kissed the top of his furry head. When she looked up, Sammi was watching her with a tender smile.

"I wish we could stay longer, but we need to be at the hospital in two hours, and I need to run home first."

Keegan nodded. "Okay. Meet you there?"

"Deal."

"Hey, Sammi?" Keegan called as Sammi turned toward the parking lot. "This was fun."

"It really was." There was a beat, then Sammi gave her a quick wave. "See you in a bit."

Keegan watched her go, and her body reacted in two ways. It tingled a bit as she watched Sammi's very shapely ass in her jeans, thought about her hands on it. And her heart gave what was now becoming a familiar squeeze, an ache of absence.

"You okay?" It was Lisa, who was there to answer questions from people about adopting the dogs. She wore a white knit hat with a pom-pom on top and a black and white jacket. Her cheeks were pink, and her eyes sparkled, probably at the possibility of finding homes for some of the animals.

"Yeah. Just rethinking my life choices." She gave Lisa a grin, only half joking.

"Oh, honey, been there, done that, got the T-shirt."

They laughed together.

❖

Okay, yeah, that was amazing. And also a lot.

The thought ran through her head on a loop as her brain replayed images of Keegan, reminded her what it felt like to sit so close to her, how warm she was, that smile, her smell, her touch. All of it was *so much*, and it had her freaking out a bit, so she wandered across the street to try to take her mind off of it all before she had to meet Keegan again.

Which turned out not to be the place to go for that.

"How was the parade?" her mother called from the living room, raising her voice to be heard over the whirring of the KitchenAid mixer her grandmother was using.

"Great. Lots of people. Chilly, but not awful." Sammi unzipped her coat.

"Last event of the fundraiser today, huh?" was the first thing her grandmother said when she turned off the mixer.

"Yup. What kind?" Sammi asked as she peered over her grandma's shoulder. "Please say molasses."

"Molasses, and you—*get*," her grandma replied, playfully swatting at Sammi's arm as she stuck a finger in the bowl of batter. "They're for my dog walking crew."

"But they're my favorite," she said.

"Is my daughter whining about cookies?" her mother asked, coming into the kitchen.

"Always," said her grandmother. "And I haven't even put the first batch in yet."

"Guess I have to hang out, then," Sammi said with a grin, draping her coat over the back of a chair and preparing to help.

"So, today is the pediatric wing at the hospital?" Her mother got herself a glass of water and sat at the small table in the corner.

Sammi nodded as she laid the silicone mat down on the cookie sheet and helped scoop batter on evenly like her grandmother had taught her.

"And how are you feeling about that?" her mom asked.

"You sound like you're my therapist," she said.

"Do you need one?" her mom asked.

"Mom. Geez." When she glanced up, both her mother and grandmother were looking at each other and grinning. "Oh, you two are so funny."

They laughed at her expense for a moment, but then her mother grew serious. "Honey, we just worry. We see how you've been around Keegan, and while your grandmother would love nothing more than to shoot Cupid's arrows into the both of you, have you fall in love and ride off into the sunset, happily ever after, I'm a little more practical."

Her grandmother scoffed at that but continued to spoon cookie batter without comment.

"Yeah?" Sammi asked. "And what do *you* want?"

"I want you to protect your heart," her mom said, and the simple sincerity in her voice nearly brought tears to Sammi's eyes.

"Hey, I want that, too," her grandma said, looking indignant.

"Please, Ma. If it was up to you, you'd have them married off and pregnant by this time next year."

"Pregnant?" Sammi echoed, surprised.

"Only if you want," her grandma said, stroking a placating hand down her arm.

The conversation devolved from there, joking and teasing taking over, and Sammi was glad for that. She stuck around long enough to snag a few warm cookies, then headed back home to get ready for the hospital. There had been no more discussion about Keegan, but as she changed her shirt to something less heavy, she recalled her mother giving her a hug as she'd left their house. She'd held her tightly, then placed a hand on Sammi's chest.

"Take care of this, okay? That's all I ask."

It seemed like such a simple request, didn't it?

❖

They'd been instructed to meet at the hospital, rather than at Junebug Farms, because Trent would need special clearance to get the dogs in. They'd come through a specific entrance, and he wanted them to meet him there.

It was the last event of this fundraising adventure, and Keegan felt a bittersweetness about it as she walked through the parking garage of the hospital, her steps echoing off the concrete walls. After all, it was the holiday season, and she had many, many other things she could be doing with her time. Christmas shopping. Wrapping gifts. Baking cookies. Attending parties. Okay, maybe she hadn't been invited to any parties, but she could throw one, couldn't she? Maybe? If she had more time? At the same time, though, she would miss these things. She'd miss the dogs for sure. She'd miss Trent and Grace and Evan a bit.

And she'd miss Sammi.

She'd miss Sammi like crazy, and that was a revelation she hadn't really expected when this had all started.

"Hey, Keegan." Evan's voice sounded from behind her, and she turned to see him and Grace coming up behind her.

"Hi, guys," she said, craning her neck to look behind them, but not seeing any sign of Sammi.

"I think she's already here," Grace said, a knowing smile on her face.

"Who?" Keegan asked.

Grace merely tilted her head and continued to smile.

She was right. When they arrived at the entrance where Trent asked them to meet him and the dogs, Sammi was already there, squatting down, loving on a Lab mix with golden fur and sweet, sweet brown eyes that Trent said was named Luna. When Sammi glanced up and met Keegan's gaze and said hi, her smile was so wide and bright, it warmed Keegan up from the inside.

"And this is Rocky," Trent was saying, yanking her out of her head and forcing her attention away from Sammi. At least for a second. She met Trent's eyes, and he smiled at her, holding out a leash.

Rocky was an adorable dog that was clearly not a purebred. He was all black, with slightly wonky ears where one stood straight up and the other stuck out to the side. His tail was curly and his chest was barrel-like, and he couldn't have weighed more than twenty pounds. His eyes were a soft brown, and when he looked into Keegan's, she felt like he'd looked into her soul, like a *whoosh* went through her bloodstream. It was the strangest feeling in the best of ways.

"Oh wow," she said quietly, but Trent heard.

"I know, right? He's something." He bent down to snap red vests on both dogs that said *Service Dog* on them.

Grace had her phone out and was scrolling through what must have been her notes. "Okay, we've got about a dozen kids to see. All are pretty sick, but a couple are..." She grimaced.

"Really sick," Keegan filled in, and Grace nodded. She glanced at Sammi, who was nodding.

"All right. Let's see if we can bring them a little holiday cheer, canine style."

For the next two hours, they went from hospital room to hospital room with the dogs, talking to the kids and their parents, wishing them a Merry Christmas. Both Luna and Rocky seemed to be calming forces. Luna would set her chin gently on the bed next to the patient and wait to be petted. Rocky was small enough that he could be set directly onto beds with the kids. There were so many hugs and kisses and pets and giggles, Keegan had a hard time believing she was lucky enough to get to witness them all.

"The joy the dogs are bringing to these kids is..." She shook her head in wonder as she spoke softly to Sammi.

"It's something to behold, isn't it?" Sammi asked.

They stood next to the bed of a young boy with a brain tumor who was scheduled for surgery the next day, three days before Christmas. Keegan watched the boy's mother as she smiled and joked with him while Rocky lay next to him, and she couldn't imagine what must be going on in the poor woman's head.

"This is amazing, what you're doing," the woman said, her eyes soft as she gazed toward Keegan and Sammi. Grace and Evan were also there, Evan being subtle about the photos he was taking, Grace jotting notes on her phone. Trent hung in the background, there to make sure the dogs were good. "It's hard on these kids to not be home for the holidays."

"Hard on their parents, too, I bet," Keegan said, her smile tender.

"Yeah. True." The woman gave a sad smile back. "Thank you for bringing Rocky. Calvin loves dogs so much." She stroked her son's head. "But with all the back and forth to the hospital lately, we just don't have the time or energy right now."

"Once I'm better, though," Calvin said, not looking at his mom as he continued to pet Rocky's soft head. His mom nodded, even as her eyes filled with unshed tears. Keegan swallowed hard, and a glance at Sammi told her the mom wasn't the only one on the verge of tears.

"How about we take Luna on to the next room and let Trent and Rocky hang with Cal for a while," Grace suggested, as if she knew they needed out of that room. Maybe she did as well.

Both of them nodded, then said temporary good-byes to Calvin and his mom before heading out into the hallway, Sammi leading Luna on her leash. Once in the hall, Sammi stopped, her hand on the wall.

"You okay?" Keegan asked, a hand on Sammi's arm.

Sammi nodded, and Keegan could see her throat move as she swallowed. "Just need a minute."

"Sure. Take your time." Keegan waved Grace and Evan on to the next room, but stayed close while Sammi took a few deep breaths and got control of her emotions, and something about the fact that she needed to do that squeezed Keegan's heart. Luna sat patiently waiting at Sammi's feet, and a moment later, Sammi blew out a breath. "Good?"

"Yeah. Thanks. That was…" Sammi shook her head.

"A lot. I know."

"Yeah." Sammi glanced at her, gratitude written all over her face.

Keegan smiled and squeezed her arm. "Come on."

The next room housed a young girl named Britney, who had just been wheeled down for an MRI. "Bad timing," Grace said, but a nurse in the room shook her head.

"No, you're okay. She should be back in about fifteen minutes. You're welcome to wait." Her gaze fell on Luna. "Well, hello there, beautiful." She squatted down and loved all over the dog for a moment while the four of them decided to wait.

"I'm gonna go find a vending machine," Evan said. "I'm starving."

"I'll go with you," Grace said. "You guys want anything?"

"Thanks, but I'm still full of my grandmother's molasses

cookies," Sammi said. "I'd have brought you some, but she threatened to take several of my fingers."

Grace made a yikes face as Keegan barked a laugh and said to her, "Please. If you met her grandmother, you'd know that this is just some poor excuse she made up for hogging all the cookies for herself."

Sammi gasped in feigned horror as Grace's laughter followed her out of the room and down the hall, Evan trailing after her.

And then it was just the two of them. And Luna, who, as if she understood they were now in a waiting period, stretched her front paws out and slid down to the floor with a soft exhale.

Sammi swallowed loudly enough that Keegan heard it.

"You okay?" she asked.

"Yeah." Sammi nodded, swallowed again, then turned to her. "I kinda wanted to address Sunday."

"Sunday?"

"Yeah. After the sledding."

Keegan frowned. "After the sledding..." She tapped a finger against her lips, the universal sign for *thinking*.

Sammi cleared her throat. "Yeah. Um. The...the kiss?"

Keegan burst out laughing. "Yeah, I knew what you meant."

A whoosh of air was expelled from Sammi's lungs. "Jesus Christ, what are you trying to do to me?" And then she was laughing, too.

"I'm sorry. You were just too cute—so very deer in the headlights—not to mess with."

"Awesome. Thanks." But Sammi stayed smiling, much to Keegan's relief.

"And okay, let's address the kiss." And she was surprised by how matter-of-factly the words came out of her mouth. "You wanna go first?"

The deer in the headlights was back, and Keegan laughed again, but then Sammi broke. "Just kidding. Sure, I can go." She inhaled slowly, tucked her dark hair behind one ear, and seemed to be organizing her thoughts. "I think..." She cleared her throat again, and her nerves just made her cuter to Keegan. "I think I was really surprised by it. I mean, don't get me wrong, it was amazing. And I was also thinking about it, and I probably would have leaned in if you hadn't." She looked toward the window of the hospital room, but Keegan somehow knew she wasn't quite done yet. Then Sammi glanced down at her feet and said, "I guess I was just surprised after what happened last year." And then she gave one nod, as if punctuating that she was finished.

Keegan let out a breath. Not exactly a sigh, but similar. "Yeah, I get that." She wanted to talk to Sammi but hadn't really expected they'd get into all the details here in the hospital room of a sick young girl, yet here they were. "As for last year..." She cleared her throat, braced her body, and dove in. "I just never got past it. I couldn't get past that moment." Whew. Okay. Good. It was out. Thank God.

She didn't look at Sammi right away. The truth was, she was afraid to. And then Sammi squatted down to pet Luna, not saying anything. Keegan watched her hand as she stroked the yellow fur. Sammi had great hands. She'd always thought so, and she found herself almost mesmerized by the rhythmic movement...

"Here we are." The nurse's voice broke through the near trance Keegan had been in, as she entered the room pushing a wheelchair occupied by a person Keegan could only assume was Britney.

Her assumptions were confirmed when the girl threw her hand—the one that wasn't in a shoulder sling—up in the air and exclaimed, "It's Britney, bitch," before being gently chided by the nurse.

Grace and Evan were right behind them, Grace laughing and Evan recording on his phone, and the rest of their discussion would have to wait. Keegan stifled her sigh.

Britney turned out to be a riot and a half. She was twelve and had been snowboarding two days before when she took a bad spill, or "bit the cannoli," as she'd described it, shattering her collarbone, tearing up her rotator cuff, and suffering a concussion. The MRI was to make sure there wasn't anything sneaky going on internally, and she was due to have surgery on her shoulder in the next day or two. She had a clear and obvious crush on Evan but also fell instantly in love with Luna. Because how could you not?

Keegan watched as she and Sammi got into a very in-depth discussion about snowboarding.

"I didn't know you snowboarded," she said to Sammi.

"Not as much as I used to, but yeah." To Britney, she asked, "Which run were you on?"

The two of them talked and joked and compared notes, and all the while, Britney stroked Luna's fur. Maybe it was because Britney was twelve or maybe it was because Keegan had been around kids her entire adult life, but every so often, she'd notice a little flash of emotion that would zip across the girl's face. Fear. Worry. Sadness. She was putting on a good show and a brave face, but Keegan could see that, just under the surface, Britney was terrified. And talking to Sammi about snowboarding seemed to help, seemed to change those zaps to small pings. It was something to watch.

She didn't know how much time had passed before Trent came in with Rocky and a nurse and announced quietly that visiting hours were coming to a close, and it was time to get the dogs back home.

"Oh, I hope somebody adopts her," Britney said, wrapping her good arm around Luna's neck. She whispered close to her ear, "Thanks for visiting me. You made me feel better." As if she could understand, Luna gave Britney's cheek a swipe with her tongue.

"I took some great shots," Evan told her. "She'll get snapped up soon, I bet."

"Good luck with your surgery," Sammi said, pointing at Britney. "Do what the doctor tells you, okay? All the exercises. All the PT."

"I will." Britney bumped the fist Sammi held out to her. "Chloe Kim rules."

"Yeah, she does."

They gathered all their things together—bags, dogs, phones—and the five of them, plus the dogs, headed for the parking garage. They came to Sammi's car first.

"This has been great, guys," she said, hugging Grace, then Evan, then Trent. "I had so much fun. I hope Jessica gives us a report of how it went, if it was worth it." She bent down to stroke each dog, and dropped a kiss on each of their furry heads. Then she stood up, hugged Keegan quickly, and turned away to get in her car.

She never looked at Keegan in the face once.

CHAPTER TWELVE

I honestly don't know what happened." Keegan sighed and sipped her Bloody Mary as she sat across the table from Shannon. She shook her head and gazed off into the restaurant, which was packed for its annual Christmas brunch. "Good thing we got our reservations early, huh? This place is a zoo."

"No, no," Shannon said, setting down her mimosa in exchange for her fork, which she pointed at Keegan before stabbing a roasted potato. "Don't change the subject. What exactly did you say?"

"The truth. I told her the truth."

"Which was?"

Keegan sighed. "That night last year. I haven't been able to get past it. That's what I told her." She sipped. "And then people came in, and she bonded with this snowboarder kid, and then we all left, and she jumped in her car with barely a word, and I haven't heard from her since."

"You texted?" Shannon asked.

Keegan gave her a look that said *Duh*.

"More than once?"

"I mean, a couple times, but I didn't want to look desperate, you know?"

"Or stalkery."

"Or that. I have my pride." She moved a few pieces of fruit around with her fork but didn't eat any of them. "I just don't understand."

"Maybe it was too much for her," Shannon said. "Maybe you just need to give her a little time to absorb?"

It wasn't a terrible suggestion. Keegan could admit that. She took her sister's words and put them in her back pocket. She could decide later if she wanted to analyze them.

Besides, she had lots of things to do. Christmas was in three days. She was out to brunch with her sister, then they were headed back to their mom's to make cookies. It was a tradition that Keegan loved, and she wasn't about to let her stupid brain ruin it for her. She needed to set this whole thing aside, at least for now. What more could she do, right?

❖

Mia hated seeing her granddaughter like this. Quiet. Pensive. A little depressed. Sammi hadn't wanted to talk about it. She just came over and plopped herself onto Mia's couch to watch the Christmas movie they had on. Every so often, Maggie would meet Mia's gaze over Sammi's head, silently battling over which of them should say something.

"You wanna talk about it?" Maggie finally asked.

"Talk about what?" Sammi asked without looking at her.

Maggie rolled her eyes, and Mia stifled a chuckle. "The reason you're here on our couch and sighing every five minutes?"

Sammi began to push to her feet. "I can go."

"Oh, sit your ass down," Maggie said, but lightly, teasingly. Sammi sat. "We're just making sure you're okay."

"I'm fine." This time, she lay down on the couch and pulled the blanket off the back of it to cover herself up. It reminded Mia of the first time Sammi got her heart broken in high school. She'd spent the next several days curled up on the couch, watching television—though not actually watching, Mia suspected—under a blanket.

She got up and headed into the kitchen, then returned a few minutes later with a plate of the molasses cookies she'd saved for Sammi, and a glass of homemade eggnog. She set them down on the coffee table in front of Sammi's face and said, "I even grated fresh nutmeg on the eggnog." When Sammi looked up at her, she smiled.

"Thanks, Grams." Sammi pushed herself to sitting and reached for a cookie. She took a bite and gave a little half-hearted smile of approval before sighing. Then she sipped the eggnog, and her eyes went wide as she looked toward Mia.

"And possibly a little Jameson in addition to the nutmeg."

Sammi burst out laughing. It was clear she couldn't help it. "You really are the best, Grams."

"I just don't like seeing you this way, kiddo."

Another sigh, and Sammi nodded slowly. "It's okay. I'm fine."

Mia didn't know the details. Sammi hadn't given any. Just that she'd talked with Keegan, and there was now clarity, and that seemed to be that. She decided to change the subject.

"So. How do you feel about going with me to bring Hulk home for Christmas?"

That got Sammi's attention, and she sat up fully. "What? Seriously?"

Maggie was just as surprised, if her suddenly wide eyes were any indication. "Um, what?"

"Oh, Mom, he's a great dog. Almost as great as Beckett."

Mia shrugged and shook her head. "I can't stop thinking about him. He's getting depressed being stuck in there. He's enormous. He's old. Nobody's looked at him. And I love the giant." She looked from Sammi to Maggie and back, both of them smiling at her like they'd known all along things would go this way, and she held up a finger. "It's just to foster him over the holiday. I can't stand the idea of him being alone for Christmas." She turned her gaze toward Maggie, who didn't look completely convinced but threw up her arms in defeat anyway.

"Fine. It can't hurt to foster for a bit."

"I am one hundred percent down for this." Sammi stood up, and her eyes were actually bright for the first time since she'd arrived, and that assured Mia that this had been the right move. "Let's go get him."

They were quiet on the drive to Junebug Farms. Mia let Sammi drive, as it was snowing gently and it made Sammi feel better if she was behind the wheel and not Mia. That was fine. It gave Mia an opportunity to observe her granddaughter, to watch the face she'd known for thirty-four years, since the moment her first breath was taken.

Sammi was a person who processed everything internally. When something bothered her, she rolled it around in her head, let it marinate, rarely wanted to talk things out until she was ready. And if you knew her the way Mia did, you let her have that time. Maggie struggled with that, often tried to force Sammi to talk, but Mia knew better.

"What's going on in that beautiful head of yours, hmm?" she asked as Sammi turned them down the road where the shelter was.

Sammi inhaled a slow, big breath. "I'm thinking a few things. First, you and I both know this isn't a case of fostering. Hulk is never coming back here. He's gonna live with you, and I hope I get to watch you try to break that to Mom." She turned her grin toward Mia, who smiled back at her, but said nothing. "And second, you've inspired me. I think I'm going to ask about adopting Beckett."

Mia clapped her hands in delight. "Yay! That's fantastic. I'm so glad."

"Not sure we should drive them home together, though. And I might not be able to get him right away anyway. Might take a couple of days. But I'm pulling the trigger."

"Finally," Mia said. She knew Sammi had been heading this way. Again, it took her granddaughter time to work through things. But she always did.

Inside, Junebug Farms was surprisingly busy for a Sunday afternoon. But it was also only two days until Christmas, so folks who were adopting pets for the holiday were ready to take them home. The big tree in front of the window was lit up in celebration. Small children ran around the giant expanse of the lobby while their parents filled out paperwork at the horseshoe-shaped front desk. The soundtrack of barking dogs was louder than usual, and Mia waved to the women behind the desk and led Sammi into the dog wing.

The second they pushed open the door, the barking increased exponentially. Mia was used to it, but Sammi faltered for a split second, then shot her a sheepish grin.

"Loud in here," she said unnecessarily.

"Tell me about it." Mia marched them straight down the hall to Lisa's desk. And of course, she was working. The poor girl put in almost as many hours as Jessica and was just as dedicated to the shelter.

"I'm gonna go say hi to Beckett," Sammi said and headed down the hallway.

"What are you doing here?" Lisa asked, moving her gaze to her computer screen. "I don't have you on the schedule..."

"That's because I'm not scheduled today." Mia smiled at her. "I'd like to take Hulk home. If that's okay."

Lisa couldn't hide her surprise, which instantly morphed into delight. "Oh, Mia, that's great."

"I can't stand the thought of him being alone for Christmas." It was the same thing she'd said to her family, and it was the truth.

"Poor guy's been really low-key lately." Lisa's tone was knowing, and Mia could only imagine how much sadness she'd witnessed in her years at the shelter. "You wanna foster him?"

"Let's put that down for now." She said nothing more, and Lisa's expression of understanding was exactly what she needed.

"Say no more." Lisa rifled through a couple baskets on her desk. "Looks like I'm out of the right forms. Let me go grab some more. You won't have to jump through all the usual hoops, since we all know you better than we know our own families. Be right back." She headed toward the door to the main lobby.

Mia glanced to her right to find Sammi standing in front of a kennel halfway down the strip. Just standing there. She walked down to meet her and immediately understood her stricken face.

A big red sign that said ADOPTED in capital letters was attached to the door.

On the other side of it, Beckett stood, nubby tail wagging, waiting expectantly for his human friend to let him out, clearly excited to see her.

"Oh, sweetie," Mia said, running her hand down Sammi's arm. "I'm so sorry."

Sammi looked like she was going to cry, and she cleared her throat and seemed to do her best to regain her composure. "No. No, it's good. He deserves a good home. You know?" She sniffled and wiped a hand under her right eye. "This is good." She cleared her throat again. "Do you think Lisa would let me see him one last time? Go in and pet him?"

"I'm sure of it."

❖

Christmas Eve was probably Keegan's favorite day of the entire year. She loved Christmas Day nearly as much, but something about Christmas Eve was more…magical to her. It seemed to carry a bit of mystery and love and a joy that no other evening did.

Their family gathering was usually fairly small, just her, her mom and dad, and Shannon, and maybe that was part of why she loved it so much. The intimacy of just their tiny family. Christmas Day would include extended family, grandparents and aunts and uncles and cousins. But Christmas Eve, it was just them. They had simple finger foods to eat, grazing all evening. They played games. They each opened a gift. Then they sat down to watch *A Christmas Story* together. And while she looked forward to the day when Christmas Eve would stretch a bit more to include the significant others of Shannon and herself, their kids, she was very happy with the way it was right now.

She sat on the floor of the living room, her back against the couch, and watched with a smile as her sister squealed with delight over a gift she opened, a sweater their mom had apparently ordered weeks ago.

"I didn't think you heard me," Shannon said, throwing her arms around their mother.

"Honey, you dropped hints every hour for a solid week," their mom replied. "There was no way *not* to hear you."

"You okay, kiddo?" her dad asked quietly, dropping a hand onto Keegan's shoulder from the couch where he sat.

She nodded as she glanced up at him. "Yeah. I'm good. I think I'm gonna take a walk, though." She pushed to her feet and could feel the eyes on her. "You guys," she said with a soft chuckle. "*I'm fine.* I promise. I just need a little air, and it's such a nice night out."

"Want me to go with?" Shannon asked, but Keegan smiled and shook her head.

"No, I'm good." Slipping her arms into her coat, she added, "I won't be gone long. Just need some air. Don't start the movie without me." She pointed a finger at her mom. The three of them were terrible at hiding their worry about her, but she shrugged it off and headed out into the snow.

The night was gorgeous, a picture-perfect Christmas Eve right out of a movie, complete with fluffy snowflakes falling slowly and quietly to the ground. She pulled on her hat and mittens and began to walk, knowing exactly where she was headed.

Silence was the other beautiful thing about Christmas Eve. The blessed quiet. As a person who taught small children for a living, she was surrounded by noise on the daily. Not even just screaming or shouting, but volume. Schools were not quiet, nor were children, even when they spoke at their regular volume—*loud*. Add in staff meetings and parent-teacher conferences, and it often seemed like endless noise. She had weekends, yes, but she would still take any chance she could to immerse herself in glorious silence.

Like now.

The street was lit up with streetlights and Christmas lights, and driveways were filled with the extra cars of visitors and holiday guests, but there was nobody on the sidewalks, and the road itself was quiet. It felt like there was nothing but Keegan, the falling snow, and the soft crunch of her boots.

She turned the corner and walked past three houses in a row with spectacular holiday displays. One was completely outlined in white lights—doors, roofline, windows, trees, everything. It was gorgeous. The next one had at least eight inflatable light-up yard decorations, everything from a snowman to Buzz Lightyear wearing a Santa hat. The third had a life-size animatronic Santa with his sleigh and eight reindeer on the roof. Keegan stopped and stared in wonder at how incredibly lifelike it was, and she thought about how much some of her students would love it.

The longer she walked, the calmer she felt, and for that, she was grateful. By the time she reached McInerny Park and laid eyes on the Christmas tree, lit up there in the town center, all multicolored lights and simple ornaments, she was feeling better. And by the time she'd walked a few more feet to the gazebo, she felt more relaxed than she had since yesterday when she'd been with—

"Sammi." The word of surprise was out of her mouth before she could catch it, because there she was. Right there in the gazebo. Sammi sat there, inside the white wooden structure, protected from the snow and all alone. She wore a black puffy coat and a red knit hat with a pom-pom on top, and her hands were tucked into her pockets. When she turned and met Keegan's gaze, her astonishment was clear.

"What are you doing here?" Sammi asked, and mixed in with her surprise was definite joy. Her smile said as much.

Keegan shrugged as she climbed the four stairs and stepped under the roof and out of the falling snow. "Just wanted some quiet time."

"Oh." Sammi's smile faltered, and she started to stand. "I can go if you—"

"You stop that," Keegan said, slapping playfully at her arm, then grew serious. "I'm glad you're here. Stay."

They sat down together, side by side, and were quiet for a long moment.

"I love this," Sammi whispered. "It's so peaceful."

"Isn't it? I feel like, if you listen really hard, you can almost hear the snowflakes when they land. Like a soft *sss*."

They were quiet for a minute or two, and then Sammi said, "Oh yeah. You can." She reached down by her feet, and that's when Keegan noticed she had a large Yeti with her.

"What's that?"

"Hot chocolate." Sammi opened the drinking tab and handed it to her.

Keegan took a sip, and it was thick and creamy and warm and sweet and, "Oh my God, that's good."

"Made it myself."

"Seriously? How did I not know of your status as an expert hot chocolate craftsman?"

"There's a lot you don't know about me."

"Valid." A beat went by. Another. And yeah, she was gonna say it. *Damn it.* "I mean, I wanted to know more. So…not for lack of trying."

She felt more than saw Sammi squint at her. "How do you figure?"

This time, Keegan did look at her. "Um…were you not there the other day when I kissed you? And then when we were talking about it at the hospital?" What in the world was Sammi saying? How was kissing her not a signal that maybe she'd like to get to know her more?

"But you said you hadn't been able to get past what happened last year." Sammi's voice was firm, almost as if she was trying to temper her anger or something. "You said *I just never got past it. I couldn't get past that moment.* That's exactly what you said."

"Yes. That's what I said because that's what I meant."

"So, if that moment was so bad, why would I think you'd want to try again?" Judging by her expression, Sammi's anger had morphed into confusion. Which was a relief to Keegan because she was utterly lost.

"What? What do you mean *so bad*? That night was so wonderful, and it was also crazy intense because my feelings for you were through the roof, and it was just *so fast.*" She swallowed hard, remembering the passion of that night, how it felt so new and so big, she'd been afraid it would swamp her like a tidal wave. "And no, I didn't handle it well. In fact, I handled it in the worst possible way I could. I ran. It was just…*so much*. It overwhelmed me. And I ran." Saying it out loud made it even worse than it had felt at the time. Worse than it had felt in the subsequent weeks and months when she'd first avoided Sammi's texts, then answered them, but in a purely platonic way until Sammi had gotten the hint.

"Wait. Your feelings for me?" Sammi's voice was soft, just above a whisper, and her eyes had gone round as the red and green balls that hung on the town Christmas tree behind them.

"Yeah."

"I…but…my God, why didn't you say something?" Sammi's eyes stayed almost comically wide, and Keegan laughed softly, despite knowing this was not the time to be laughing.

"Because I didn't know how? Because I was afraid? Because I'm an idiot?" She held up her hands, out of answers. "Take your pick."

Sammi simply sat there looking a combination of stunned and confused.

"I know," Keegan said. "I know, and I'm so sorry. I'd come out of a relationship that left me kinda battered, and I'd promised myself—I'd vowed—that I'd take my time the next time, that I wouldn't jump in, as I tend to do. That I would take my time and step carefully and look before I leaped and all those stupid clichés." She looked down at her mittens, focused on the colors of the marled yarn—blues and greens and ivories. "And then you came along, and there I was, diving in headfirst because everything was so good. Everything just fit. And…I panicked."

Sammi had sat quietly, taking her words in. She had pulled red mittens that matched her hat out of her pockets and pushed her hands into them. Now, like Keegan, she stared at them for a long time. So long that Keegan started to wonder if she was going to speak at all. Maybe she wasn't. Maybe this was all just ridiculous. Maybe Keegan had had her chance a year ago, she'd blown it in spectacular fashion, and she needed to leave Sammi alone and move on with her life.

Still, she sat.

Still, Sammi sat.

Still, the snow fell.

Finally, Sammi spoke. "I want to tell you you're a fool."

"I know." Keegan nodded, her eyes on her mittens. "I know."

"No." Sammi waited until Keegan met her gaze. "I *want* to tell you that because I'm kind of annoyed that we've wasted an entire year. But I can't."

"You can't?" What in the world? "Why not?"

Sammi shrugged as she blew out a breath, the vapor floating off and disappearing. "Because I get it. Because everything you said makes sense to me."

"It does?" Did her eyes bug out of her head? Because it felt like they might have, as shocked as she was by Sammi's words.

"That your feelings were too big? Too much? That you got overwhelmed? Of course it does. That's something that could easily happen to anybody."

Keegan just blinked at her. This was not the response she'd expected.

"Now, that being said, am I kind of irritated at the way you handled things? Abso-fucking-lutely."

Keegan snorted a laugh. She couldn't help it. "Understood. Definitely. I'm so sorry."

"I mean, you had plenty of time, lots of opportunities to just tell me. Right? But you friend-zoned me."

Keegan sighed. "I did."

"Ugh." Sammi shook her head. "Such a fool."

"It's true. A fool who would like more hot chocolate, please."

Sammi handed over the Yeti without comment, and Keegan drank it down, letting the warm sweetness fill her up.

They sat quietly for a long while, just listening to the snowflakes.

"What do we do now?" Keegan asked the question, even though she was slightly afraid of the answer. Sammi was well within her rights to shrug and walk away. Keegan hoped she didn't, but if she did, she'd have to accept it. This was her fault.

"I think we start over." Sammi's voice was clear and matter-of-fact.

"Yeah?"

"Mm-hmm."

"Okay. How?"

"What if you come to my house tomorrow night? After you celebrate with your family. Do you have the time for that?"

Keegan turned to look at her, and she waited until Sammi made eye contact. When she did, it felt like something clicked into place. That's how it always was with her. Why had she been so afraid before? "Sammi, you could ask me to fly to Portugal tomorrow because you're going to be there, and I'd make the time."

A beat passed while she simply watched Sammi smile tenderly before she spoke. "Sadly, I'll just be in my own little house, which is not in Portugal, but on Sycamore Street right here in Northwood."

"Sycamore Street sounds perfect."

"Okay." Sammi's grin grew wider.

"Okay." Keegan felt lighter. "I should probably get back to my parents' before they send out a search party."

"Same."

They stood together, and Keegan handed the Yeti back to Sammi. "Thanks for sharing your hot chocolate."

"Sure."

They took the steps down into the snow, Keegan's previous footsteps almost filled in. She turned to face Sammi, who looked so fucking gorgeous in her winter clothes with the snow falling softly around her that it took Keegan's breath for a moment. "Tomorrow, then?"

"Tomorrow, then," Sammi said, and then she leaned forward and pressed her lips to Keegan's. She didn't linger, but she was there long enough for Keegan to feel the softness, the warmth, the sweet hint of chocolate. "Merry Christmas, Keegan."

"Merry Christmas, Samantha." She watched as Sammi turned and headed in the opposite direction. She watched the movement of her shoulders, the sway of her hips. She watched for a long time, until Sammi's voice rang out in the quiet of the night.

"Stop staring at my ass."

Keegan burst out laughing.

CHAPTER THIRTEEN

Christmas Day couldn't be over fast enough. And Sammi never felt that way. Ever. It was her favorite day of the year. She looked forward to it so much, and once it arrived, she wanted it to last much longer than its disappointing twenty-four hour limit.

But not today.

Today, she ripped through her presents. Today, she ate as quickly as she possibly could. Today, she chatted and hugged and celebrated, because she *was* happy. It still was her favorite day. But she also couldn't wait until she could safely make an exit without garnering suspicion or hurting anybody's feelings.

It took fucking forever.

For. Ever.

But it finally came.

Six o'clock. That's the time she'd given herself, because Keegan had texted that she'd be over by seven. She pushed her chair back from the dining room table where she was watching her grandmother, her mom, her grandmother's friend Angelo, and her uncle Jack playing poker. She'd folded long ago, then bowed out, asking just to watch. Mostly because she couldn't concentrate on the game knowing she was going to be seeing Keegan before long.

"All right. I'm heading across the street." She said it firmly, hoping her tone would prohibit any argument.

"Okay, honey," her mom said, not looking up from her hand of cards.

"Thanks for losing to us," Angelo teased, then tossed her a wink.

"Come over tomorrow morning for French toast and mimosas, if you'd like," her grandmother said. "There will be plenty." Hulk was crashed out on the floor at her feet, apparently exhausted from his first Christmas with the Sorensons.

She went around the table and gave everybody a squeeze, wished them Merry Christmas, told her grandma she'd grab her gifts tomorrow, and bent to give Hulk a kiss on his giant head. He barely opened his eyes. Then she stepped into her boots, donned her coat, and ran across the cul-de-sac to her own house, the whole time thanking her lucky stars that nobody had tried to guilt her into staying longer.

She'd done a small bit of cleaning that morning when she'd gotten up, but now she zipped around the house, putting things away, tossed a couple dirty dishes into the dishwasher, and turned on some instrumental holiday music on the speaker. Then she opened a bottle of pinot noir to let it breathe, and also put a bottle of chardonnay in the fridge. 'Cause options.

A glance at her watch told her it was six fifty. She ran upstairs and decided to leave her jeans on but changed her shirt, pulling off her Christmas hoodie with the big Rudolph on the front and exchanging it for a white tank top and a red-and-green flannel button-down, which she left open. Still Christmassy, but a tiny bit neater than the hoodie. She gave her teeth a quick brush and tidied her hair, then went back into the bedroom for a spritz of her favorite scent.

Headlights waved through across the ceiling and then off.

"Oh God, she's here."

She said the words into the empty room, feeling that funny, fluttery feeling in her stomach—that combination of excitement and anxiety. She swallowed down the nerves, gave herself a quick once-over in the mirror, and headed down to the front door, then pulled it open.

Keegan stood there, looking red-cheeked and gorgeous in her

white coat and green hat. Her eyes sparkled, her hair hung down from the hat, and her smile was wide.

In one hand, she held a bag. In the other, one end of a leash.

"Merry Christmas, Sammi."

At the other end of the leash was Beckett. His whole body started to wag when he saw her.

"What? Oh my God. Oh my God! Hi, buddy! Hi! Hi! Hi!" She knelt right down in the entryway, not caring if her knees got wet, and wrapped her arms around the dog, who was wiggling so much with excitement that it was hard to hold on to him. She finally looked up at Keegan. "I don't understand." Then she pushed to her feet. "And God, I'm sorry, come in. It's cold out."

She ushered Keegan and Beckett into the house, and Beckett seemed to know he needed to be on his best behavior. Keegan handed over the leash while she took her coat and hat off, and Beckett stayed close, gazing up at her like he'd never seen anything more wonderful in his entire doggie life.

Keegan hung her things up, and when she finally met Sammi's eyes again, Sammi raised her eyebrows. Keegan's smile was warm and sweet and it did things to Sammi. "He's yours," Keegan said simply.

"He's…" She looked at Keegan in disbelief.

"He's yours. I got tired of waiting for you to pull the trigger on something you so obviously wanted but were too hesitant to grab, so I grabbed him for you." She petted Beckett's big square head. "I ran it by your mom first, just to make sure it wasn't a mistake. I almost asked your grandma, but—no offense to her—your mom seems to be the more practical one."

Sammi laughed at that. "Facts. And no wonder she didn't try to get me to stay longer tonight," Sammi said, but she couldn't be mad at the charade. "She knew he was coming."

"She did."

"I was at the shelter yesterday with Grams, and I went to say hi to Beckett and saw the adopted sign on his kennel. I'm pretty sure I actually felt my heart crack."

Keegan frowned. "Oh God, I'm sorry about that."

Sammi waved it off with a *pfft*. "Doesn't matter, 'cause it's okay now." She got down on her knees so she could look Beckett in his soft brown eyes. "Hey, buddy. You wanna live here? With me?"

The dog wagged his whole body again, and Sammi unclipped the leash.

"Okay. Go explore. Please don't pee on stuff." She glanced up at Keegan. "But if you do, it's okay. We'll work on it." She stood back up, and they watched the dog slowly walk around the living room, sniffing things here, sniffing things there. He kept looking back, as if making sure Sammi hadn't gone anywhere. She turned to Keegan and felt a sudden lump in her throat. "Thank you, Keegan," she said softly. "So, so much."

Keegan grabbed her arm and leaned in to her. "You are so welcome."

"I got you a little something, too, but it pales in comparison," Sammi said with a soft chuckle.

"I'm just happy I'm here, to be honest."

Sammi met her gaze. "Yeah?"

"Absolutely. I've been looking forward to it all day. First time in my life I wanted Christmas Day to go faster."

Sammi barked a laugh. "Same."

"Really?"

"You have no idea." They watched Beckett for another moment. "He's doing really well."

"He is. You should show him his new yard."

"Oh, good idea."

They walked to the back door together.

❖

Adopting a dog for somebody else was a risk. Keegan had known that. But seeing the longing in Sammi's eyes every time she was with Beckett, it was so clear they were meant for each other. She'd actually adopted him a while back, just to be safe and to make sure nobody else snapped him up before Sammi finally made the decision to take him home.

She hadn't expected it to take so long.

Sammi was a person who needed a nudge every now and then. Keegan was learning this about her. And her mom had confirmed it when she'd called to ask about the dog.

"My daughter is one of the smartest, kindest, gentlest souls I know," Maggie had said. "But sometimes, she needs a little kick in the behind to get her moving." She'd said it with a laugh and a tone of great affection, and it had been a huge help in getting Keegan to take the chance. And getting Beckett out of the shelter on Christmas Day had also taken some favors.

But here they were.

And the smile on Sammi's face, the utter delight in everything about her, told Keegan it had been exactly the right thing to do. Sammi had slipped on her coat and boots and had run out into the snow, Beckett bounding behind her, and now Keegan stood inside the sliding glass door and watched them bounce and play and roll around like two small children having the time of their lives.

She'd helped herself to the wine Sammi had breathing on the counter, and now she sipped it through her smile. While she'd expected to be happy about bringing Beckett and Sammi together, she found herself feeling downright giddy as she watched them. Sammi was flat on her back in the snow, Beckett barking and bouncing around her. She didn't think his nubby tail had stopped wagging his entire back end since they'd arrived and he saw Sammi. The two of them were meant for each other.

Was it the same for her and Sammi?

Wait a minute…Slow down there, skippy. She smiled at her own racing thoughts. Why was life so complicated? Why was love so complicated? And at the use of the L-word, she slammed the door on those racing thoughts. So not ready for that. Big yikes.

She busied herself with unloading the bag she'd brought. It contained some dog bowls, a small amount of dog food, the blanket Beckett slept on in the shelter, and a couple of toys. She figured

Sammi could figure out the details of how she wanted to care for her new dog, but this stuff would tide her over. She laid a placemat down in a corner of the dining room, filled one of the bowls with water, and set both bowls on the mat. She tossed the toys into the center of the living room and draped the blanket over a chair, not sure where Sammi would want Beckett to sleep.

The sliding glass door slid open, and Beckett came bounding in, making Keegan wonder if that was going to be his method of transport from here on out: bounding. He did some zoomies around the living room, his tongue hanging out.

"I don't think he's happy at all," Keegan said.

Sammi was out of breath, her cheeks rosy, her smile huge. She toed off her boots and slipped her coat off, draping it over a chair, then crossed to Keegan without preamble and wrapped her in a tight hug. When she finally let go, she met Keegan's gaze and held it for several seconds before saying softly, "Thank you, Keegan. This—he—is the best gift I've ever gotten."

Keegan straightened up. "Seriously?"

"Seriously." And then Sammi took her face in both hands and kissed her. Soundly. Thoroughly. Softly, but not. Demandingly, but not. Just as Keegan was letting herself melt into it, Sammi pulled back. Still holding her face, she asked, "Was that okay?"

Keegan tried to speak, but her voice was hiding. She cleared her throat and tried again. "Um. Yes. Very. Very okay."

Sammi's grin was a knowing one, but all she said was, "Good."

Keegan tipped her head and watched for a moment, then poured a glass of wine for Sammi. She took the glass and her own into the living room where Beckett was now lying on his side on the carpet, breathing heavily. As soon as he saw Keegan, his nubby tail started to wag, but he didn't get up. "I think you sufficiently wiped him out."

"*For now*," Sammi said, her expression comically ominous. She indicated the couch. "Wanna sit?"

Keegan nodded, handed her the wine, and took a seat.

"You want something to eat? I have some cheese and crackers, some chips…"

"Oh God, no." Keegan held up a hand and waved. "I ate so much at my mom's. I'm gonna be full for a week."

"I feel you. My grandmother made a ham *and* a roast, mashed potatoes *and* sweet potatoes, four different pies…" Sammi dropped her head onto the back of the couch. "So. Much. Food."

That sat silently for a beat or two, sipping wine and watching Beckett's heaving breaths level off until they were normal and he was asleep.

"I don't think he's comfortable here at all," Keegan said, giving Sammi a bump with her shoulder.

Sammi shook her head. "I still can't believe you did this."

Keegan lifted a shoulder. "You needed a nudge."

"I did. It's true. I tend to overthink things."

She gasped. "What? Overthink? You?"

"Ha ha. You're very funny."

Keegan leaned in to her as they laughed, and this time, she stayed close, liking the feel of Sammi's body propping hers up. Sammi felt warm, strong, and solid, and Keegan had let a happy little sigh slip out before she'd realized it.

"I like that sound," Sammi said quietly.

"Do you?"

"I do. It sounded content. Relaxed. That's what I want you to be with me."

"Well, I am. Right now."

"Good."

There was another moment of quiet, and then Sammi started to laugh softly. It grew in volume until she was laughing outright.

"What?" Keegan said and couldn't help her own smile. "What's so funny?"

"*We* are," Sammi said, laughing harder. "Look at us. We're ridiculous. We have danced around each other for a year. *A year*. We like each other. We have chemistry. We're good together. Yet the second your feelings got big, you freaked out and ran away. And better yet, *I* didn't chase you down. What is wrong with us?" She was laughing so hard now that her eyes were wet. "You adopted me a dog for Christmas, for God's sake!"

Keegan's laughter was soft, but in minutes, it grew because, holy shit, Sammi was absolutely right. She was so right. They were officially ridiculous. And they were cracking up. Together.

Beckett lifted his head from the floor where he had sprawled and looked at the two of them like they were a couple of weirdos, which only made them laugh harder, falling against each other, tears streaming down faces. It was all so silly and so hilarious, and Keegan felt like she could breathe again for the first time in literal months.

It took a few minutes more for them to collect themselves, for the laughter to die down to chuckles and then finally stop. They still leaned against each other, sitting back on the couch and looking at the sparkling lights on Sammi's tree.

"I'd like to give this another try," Keegan said quietly. She wasn't nervous about saying it, surprisingly. She turned to meet Sammi's gaze. "What do you think?"

"I think you know that I would also like to give this another try."

Keegan sighed happily. "Good."

"But listen." Sammi turned so she was facing Keegan now, and her expression was serious. "If you feel weird or scared or freaked out in any way, you have to talk to me. Okay? None of this leaving in the middle of a make-out session never to be heard from again."

Keegan grinned sheepishly. "That's an exaggeration, but okay."

"It's not *much* of an exaggeration," Sammi muttered, turning back to face front, and Keegan laughed.

She reached for Sammi, put a hand on her upper arm until their eyes met again. "That's a fair request. I'll do my best."

"That's all I ask."

They were quiet, the only sound in the room that of Beckett's snores. "Clearly, he hates it here," Keegan said with a grin.

"Yeah, this is a disaster," Sammi deadpanned. "Obviously, I'll need to return him."

They laughed softly together, and then grew quiet again, but it wasn't uncomfortable. At some point, they shifted positions so that Keegan sat with her back against the arm of the couch, and

Sammi leaned back against her. They had a perfect view of the tree, its multicolored lights twinkling in the night. Sammi reached for a small remote on the coffee table and clicked it, turning off the lamp in the corner, so the tree was the only light in the room.

It was beautiful.

The tree, the quiet, Beckett's gentle snorfles from the floor, Sammi in her arms…if she could have stayed right here in this moment forever, Keegan wouldn't have been sad about it.

It was beautiful.

And this Christmas? It was perfect.

CHAPTER FOURTEEN

The next two days went by in a blur. Keegan had the rest of the week off, as well as the following one, but Sammi did not. In fact, she had dental surgery to perform on Friday, so she was right back in the office, and there was a lot of time spent worrying about Beckett being home alone. To help, she got herself a nanny cam so she could keep an eye on him, thinking if he got into anything or was being a nut, she could give her grandma a call and have her run over to the house.

Shockingly, every time she checked the app on her phone, Beckett was asleep. On the couch, where Sammi had initially not wanted him to be, but asleep. Nothing chewed up. Nothing peed on. No ridiculous zoomies around the house. He simply...slept.

"He's probably so exhausted from being in the shelter for so long," Keegan said on the phone Friday, when Sammi found herself with a five-minute break and just wanted to hear her voice, rather than to read typed words in a text. "I mean, you know how loud it is in there. Sleeping couldn't have been easy. Like trying to sleep in the hospital when somebody's always coming in and the noise never ends."

"That's a good point," Sammi said with a nod.

"He's got some catching up to do." She could hear the smile in Keegan's voice. She paused, then asked, "Busy day?"

"I've got one more patient to see, and then I'm done."

"And then it's the weekend. God, I love Fridays."

"Wanna go to dinner?" It was so strange to her how asking

Keegan such a question would've sent her nerves into overdrive territory a few weeks ago, but now, it was as simple as asking about the weather.

"Well, I actually have a different idea…" Keegan seemed to let the sentence hang for a moment or two, then went on. "What if we ordered in and watched a movie at your place?"

"Yeah?"

"I mean, Beckett is there. Not that we can't leave him home, but I'm sure you want to see him."

"Don't you mean *you* want to see him?" Sammi teased.

"That's what I said. *I* want to see him." Her tone made Sammi laugh.

"I think that sounds like a fantastic idea. I should be out of here by four. Come on over whenever. I'll leave the door unlocked."

She hung up the phone, very aware of the goofy grin on her face. How they'd gotten to this point so quickly was baffling, but also amazing, and she wasn't about to start questioning it. Instead, she finished with her patient, sent her staff home for the weekend, and did a few housekeeping bits of paperwork. Then she stopped at the liquor store on the way home and bought a couple bottles of wine.

When she pulled in her driveway, she checked her camera app out of curiosity. Beckett was still on the couch, but his head was up and cocked to one side, clearly listening. Then he stood up and looked out the front window where he saw her, and his nubby tail started wiggling, his entire back end shaking on the couch, and she couldn't help but grin and wave at him. Having a creature that excited to see her when she got home sent her heart soaring, and she hurried inside to love all over him.

They were still in a cuddle puddle in the middle of the living room floor when the doorbell rang, and Keegan pushed her way in.

"Ho, ho, ho, anybody home?" she asked as she toed off her boots and slipped out of her coat.

Beckett jumped up and ran to her, as excited to see her as he had been to see Sammi, and Sammi stayed sitting on the floor, watching, until they finally made their way into the room.

"He hasn't gone out yet," Sammi said, as she pushed to her feet. Without thinking about it, she leaned in and kissed Keegan. "Hi."

Keegan's cheeks blossomed a pale pink. "Hi."

One more kiss. And then another.

"I missed you today," Keegan whispered, and she couldn't have said anything sweeter. Sammi felt like she floated to the back door to let Beckett out.

Together, they decided to order a pizza, pour some cabernet, and watch a true crime documentary about a serial killer living in a residential neighborhood. Snuggled together on the couch under a blanket with Beckett on the floor close by, they watched, riveted, and when it was finished, Keegan let out a long, slow breath.

"Well. Now I'm going to have to keep a much closer eye on all my neighbors. So thanks for that, Netflix."

"Listen," Sammi said, her voice low. "The guy who lives over there?" She pointed vaguely behind her. "I hardly ever see him. He disappears for days on end. And has a *workshop* in his basement. I hear power tools running *all the time*." She widened her eyes in mock horror.

Keegan feigned a gasp. "What if he's holding women prisoner down there? And...and...dismembering them with his power tools."

They held horrified gazes and then both burst into laughter.

"He's actually an architect who goes on a lot of business trips," Sammi said through her laughter. "And he makes amazing furniture in his workshop."

"Or *so you think*," Keegan said, still chuckling, as she met Sammi's gaze.

This time, it was Keegan who leaned in for the kiss. And lingered. And lingered a little longer. She tasted sweet and salty—a little from the wine, a little from the pizza—and Sammi wanted more. She took the wineglass from Keegan's hand and set it on the coffee table, then turned back to her. She took her time, making sure to gauge Keegan's expression, looking to see if she might be getting nervous or thinking of bolting again.

But all she saw was a soft expression of welcome, so she took

Keegan's face in both hands and kissed her soundly. Tenderly. Like they had all the time in the world.

Because they did.

They kissed for a long time—or at least Sammi thought it felt like a long time—and she could've kept on until the end of time. Kissing Keegan was...so many things. Soft. Sensual. Sexy. Intriguing. Wonderful. So. Many. Things.

Eventually, they parted, and for Sammi, it was purposeful, before things got too hot and heavy. She didn't want any flashbacks or repeats of the last time. So she pressed her forehead to Keegan's and sighed happily as she smiled.

Keegan's face was flushed and her lips were a little puffier than usual, and her smile matched Sammi's as she ran her fingertips over Sammi's bottom lip. "You're a really, really good kisser," she whispered.

"Why, thank you. You're pretty damn good yourself."

"We kiss well together."

"Damn right we do."

Beckett lifted his head from the floor and looked at them as if telegraphing how ridiculous this conversation was, and it made Sammi grin.

"He's judging us," Keegan said.

"He absolutely is."

Keegan inhaled deeply and let it out. "Okay, so, I think I should go." Sammi's expression must've telegraphed something because Keegan put a hand on her arm and squeezed. "No, no. It's nothing like last time, I promise. It's just...I like this pace we have going. You know?" She glanced off into the distance as if searching for the right words. "I'm so, *so* good at jumping in. With both feet— or sometimes headfirst—and no regard for any consequences or concerns." She narrowed her eyes as she looked at Sammi. "Does that make sense?"

"Look, as long as you're not going to leave here and then disappear from my life for weeks or months, I'm perfectly happy to follow your lead." She was able to say that because of the soft look on Keegan's face. She remembered last time all too well, like it was a movie reel stuck on a loop in the back of her mind. The slight panic. The inability to look Sammi in the eye. The shame.

None of that was present now. Keegan simply looked content, and that was all Sammi needed. She pushed to her feet and held out her hand so she could pull Keegan up.

They kissed softly at the door once Keegan was in her coat and gloves, and she'd started her car remotely.

"Tomorrow?" Keegan asked quietly.

"Tomorrow." Sammi kissed her once more and then watched as she walked to her car, got in, and backed out. She sighed a happy, contented sigh. It was a gorgeous winter night. Not too cold, but not warm enough to make it wet and slushy. She called to Beckett, who trotted over to stand next to her. "How do you feel about taking a nighttime walk, huh, buddy?"

She'd spent some time at the pet store the day after Christmas and purchased a bright red coat to keep Beckett warm on walks. She strapped him into it, his harness, and his leash, got herself all bundled up, and they headed out.

She hadn't realized it was going on eleven o'clock. The stars were bright in the deep, dark sky, and her breath puffed out in clouds and dissipated in the night. The sidewalks were quiet, of course, and Christmas decorations still twinkled on houses and in yards in her neighborhood.

She hadn't really understood how peaceful it could be to walk a dog. Beckett was excellent on the leash. He stopped to sniff a lot, but Sammi didn't mind. This was thinking time, head-clearing time. And the only thought in her head was Keegan. She didn't need to be cleared out.

If you'd asked Sammi two months ago—hell, maybe even one month ago—if she thought she be where she was now, walking her dog and seeing Keegan, she'd have laughed heartily and told you that was the most outlandish question ever because *of course she wouldn't be.*

And now?

She felt her smile bloom across her face. 'Cause yeah. And now.

This slow pace they were taking didn't bother her at all. It felt healthy. Was that weird? Because it was accurate. And she couldn't remember the last time she took a consciously healthy step in a relationship. Like, ever.

This was a new Samantha Sorenson. A new Sammi for a new year.

"I like it, Beck," she said quietly. "I like it a lot."

They turned for home.

❖

"Are you coming over for New Year's Eve?" Mia's granddaughter had come over on Saturday with her new Christmas present, one with four paws and sweet brown eyes and a big block-shaped head, who wanted nothing more than to be petted and loved and to play with Hulk. Mia sat on the kitchen floor as Beckett rolled onto his back with his head in her lap like there was no one in the world he trusted more. And then Hulk whined, clearly filled with jealousy, and lay down next to Beckett, and Mia's happiness surged. "Oh my God, these dogs. How did we get so lucky?"

Sammi laughed as she took a bite of a Christmas cookie, sitting at the small round table with her mom. "Is this the last batch of these?" She held up the half-eaten cookie, and Mia nodded.

"Until next year, yup."

"Damn it." Sammi took a much smaller bite, like she was trying to make the cookie last longer, and it made her mother laugh. "Yes, I'll be over Tuesday night. Um…" She hesitated, but Mia knew exactly what she was hesitant about.

"Of course you can bring Keegan," she said before Sammi could figure out the words she wanted to use. "And please bring this granddoggie of mine. Yes, please." Her voice went up a couple octaves as she changed to baby talk, and she gave Beckett belly scratches, which only made him wiggle more. "Yes, please. He can keep Hulkie company." After a moment, she looked at Sammi and held out a hand. "All right, help your old grandmother off the floor."

"You're not old, Grams," Sammi said as she held out a hand, then pulled Mia to her feet. "You're gonna outlive us all."

Maggie barked a laugh of agreement at the same time Mia said, "Pfft."

"So, who all will be here on Tuesday?" Sammi asked, grabbing another cookie. "Is it a party?"

Mia opened a cupboard door and pulled out a box of dog treats. Sammi laughed as she caught a glimpse of several more boxes and pouches in many varieties.

"Keeping the dog treat companies in business, I see."

"Totally worth it." She grinned as she pulled out a treat and told the boys to sit. Hulk sat immediately. Beckett blinked at her a good three times, but then dropped his butt to the ground. "Good boy."

"Fine," Sammi said, laughing. "We have a little work to do." Then she glanced at her mom, who sat at the table observing in her usual quiet way. "You knew. You knew Keegan had adopted him for me."

Maggie simply smiled and sipped her coffee.

Mia shook her head with a grin as she gave Beckett a second treat, then put the box away. "That girl likes you, Samantha. I don't think you even realize how much."

"I like her, too, Grams." Sammi looked at the plate with the cookie supply that was dwindling fast. "Damn it," she whispered and grabbed another one. "You didn't answer me. Is Tuesday a party? Or just a small group?"

"It's a small party. You, Keegan, me, your mother, a couple of my dog walking friends, and their partners if they have them. That's all. Why?"

"I mean…"

And right there in her kitchen, she watched her granddaughter turn four different shades of red and shrug like she wasn't sure what to say.

"She means," Maggie said, clearly hiding a grin, "that she wants to make out with her new girlfriend at midnight, but not in front of a bunch of strangers."

"*Mom*," Sammi said with an expression of horror on her face that had both Maggie and Mia cracking up.

"But am I wrong?" Maggie asked.

"That's not the point," Sammi said, verging on whining, and Maggie and Sammi were off to the races, teasing.

Sitting in her kitchen, watching and listening to the woman who was like a daughter to her and the woman who carried her son's blood in her veins play and tease each other, was one of Mia's favorite things in the world to do. Her son had been gone for ten years, but here, in this kitchen right now, were the three women he'd loved most in the world: his mother, his wife, and his daughter. It was a bittersweet realization.

"Hey, Grams, you okay?" Sammi's voice pulled Mia out of her head to find that they were both looking at her.

She blinked rapidly, hoping the tears that had welled up in her eyes wouldn't fall, and she nodded. "I'm wonderful, honey. I'm wonderful. Come here and give your grandma a hug."

❖

The Big Feelings were back. Hard-core.

Keegan wasn't terribly surprised, because she knew herself pretty well, but that didn't mean they weren't…slightly unnerving.

"You okay, honey?" her mom asked as they worked in the kitchen. They were having a family dinner tonight, and Keegan had come over to help, now standing at the counter peeling potatoes that would end up mashed to perfection.

"Yeah," she said.

"Unconvincing." Her mom's smile was gentle and knowing and said *talk to me* without her actually having to say it.

"God, you know me well." She gave a soft chuckle at the truth of the statement.

"I'm a mother. I know when something's up with one of my kids." They were both quiet for a moment before she said, "Is it Sammi?"

Keegan nodded.

"Bad?" Her mom made a face, and Keegan smiled and shook her head.

"No. Good. Very, very good."

"What's the problem, then?"

Keegan sighed because how could she put this into words? How could she define something she didn't quite understand? "I didn't expect to be back here," was what she started with.

"Here…?" Her mom waited for clarification.

"Here where there are feelings for her."

"Oh," her mom said, drawing the word out. "I would say that it's awfully soon for those, but I know they were the problem last time, so…" She cocked her head as she met her daughter's gaze. "Maybe they never left?"

"I think that might be the case." She picked up another potato and got to peeling. She really hadn't been all in on Jules. True, she'd had her own problems, but Keegan knew she hadn't really given it her all. Maybe this was why.

"Honey, forgive me if this is a stupid thing to say, but I never understood what the problem was before. Like, you had feelings for her, but why was that bad? She seems great."

"She *is* great. She's so great." She took a deep breath, again searching for the right way to describe what she'd felt then. "I've had feelings for people before. I've been in love before. But with Sammi…" She shook her head. "It came on so fast and so hard and"—she met her mom's eyes—"honestly, Mom, it scared the shit out of me."

"Oh," her mom said and, again, drew the word out. "You didn't tell me that."

"I didn't tell *anybody* that. I was so freaked out by how strong it all felt that I just ran. I ran and tucked it all away in a box in my head, never to be dealt with again."

"Oh, Keegan," her mother said with a clearly disapproving tone, as she stopped what she was doing to give her daughter a look that matched. "That poor girl."

"I know. I know, I'm not proud of it. And now…" She let the sentence dangle unfinished.

"And now she's giving you a second chance and the feelings are back and you're afraid of hurting her again."

"Exactly." What a fucking relief to not have to explain it, to say the words out loud.

"Then don't."

"I don't want to, believe me."

"Then. Don't."

"You make it sound so easy."

Her mother again stopped what she was doing and fixed Keegan with a look, and this time, she was clearly annoyed with her kid. Keegan knew when that was the case, and it was exactly the case right now. "Listen to me. If you like this girl, then *like her*. Treat her with kindness and respect. If you don't think you can do that, then you let her go *now*. You hurt her once already. Most people don't get a second chance, you know. She must really like you."

Keegan was quiet for a moment, lost in the combination of absorbing her mother's words, feeling guilty about them, and the realization that she then spoke out loud. "I really like her, too," she said quietly.

Her mother's whole demeanor softened. "Then like her, baby. There's no rush. There's no hurry. *Feel* your feelings. They're not bad things. Okay?" Keegan met her mom's eyes with her own wet ones, and her mother pulled her into a hug. "Oh, sweetie. You have such a big heart. You always have. And sometimes, your feelings? They swamp you, like a rowboat on the ocean. It's happened your whole life, and—honestly?—it's hard for your mother to watch." She gave a sarcastic chuckle. "One of the joys of parenthood—I can't make your decisions for you." She squeezed Keegan tightly to her, and Keegan's eyes continued to well up. "Your heart is the best part of you. Listen to it, okay? Honor it."

Keegan's tears spilled over then, trailing softly down her cheeks. "I will, Mom." Her voice was barely above a whisper. "I will."

Chapter Fifteen

Keegan loved the Sorensons. If she hadn't already been pretty sure by the time she arrived at their New Year's Eve party, that night would've sealed it. Mia was her usual funny, welcoming self. Maggie was lovely, kind and soft-spoken, but a person who could come in with a zinger of a line when you least expected it and crack up the entire place. She reminded Keegan so much of Sammi, though with an element of sadness deep in her eyes.

She recognized a few of the partygoers from Junebug Farms. Angelo looked familiar, as did Beth. The other two—Carmen and Francie—were new to her, along with their plus-ones, and it rounded out into a nice group of interesting people. Not too big, not too small. Keegan was glad to be there.

Sammi stayed close, even as she did her best to help out her mother and grandmother with hors d'oeuvre and keeping folks' drinks fresh.

"You're quite the bartender," she said to Sammi after watching her make two old-fashioneds, one for Angelo and one for herself, complete with orange bitters and a piece of rind she peeled off an orange herself. "I had no idea."

"There's so much for you to learn about me," Sammi said with a sexy little twinkle in her eye.

"Oh, I can hardly wait," she said, flirting back quietly. And she meant it. Since talking with her mother on Sunday, she'd felt a bit of a shift within her that was hard to specify. But it was lovely. Firm. Determined.

Sammi shot her a grin that made her knees weak, then headed off to deliver Angelo his drink. And her knees stayed weak as she watched Sammi walk away, the sway of her hips, the shine on her dark hair, the way she smiled at Angelo as she handed over his glass, then touched hers to it in a friendly cheers.

People liked Sammi. That was something Keegan had noticed right away about her. She put people at ease, was very approachable, and people tended to feel comfortable with her from the beginning. Keegan had. It was a quality not a lot of people had. No wonder Sammi's practice was thriving. People felt safe and comfortable with her.

Keegan felt safe and comfortable with her, too. And also? Super turned-the-hell-on right now. She closed her eyes and used her wineglass to hopefully cover the grin and maybe some of the blush that she felt heat up her face. When she opened them again, Sammi was looking at her and gesturing for her.

"Hey," Sammi said when she was next to her. "You've met Angelo, yeah?" At Keegan's nod, Sammi went on. "He says Jessica is super happy with the donations that have come from the holiday fundraiser."

"Oh, really?" Keegan said. "That's great. I'm so glad to hear it."

"And," Angelo added, taking a sip of his drink and making a very happy face of approval before he continued, "you two have gotten some great commentary. Not sure if you followed along on socials, but lots of good comments."

"I didn't look a ton," Keegan admitted. "I was kind of afraid of what people would say." She glanced at Sammi. "Being a queen and queen."

Angelo scoffed. "Well, there was certainly some of that because people are assholes, but it was overwhelmingly positive, according to Jessica. You should be proud of yourselves." Then he looked over Sammi's shoulder. "Oh, I think your grandma is summoning me. Later, girls." And he and his old-fashioned headed toward the kitchen.

Sammi raised her own old-fashioned. "Here's to the two queens and the money they helped raise for homeless animals."

"I will most definitely drink to that." Keegan touched her glass to Sammi's and they sipped. Sammi's eyes were on hers, and they held. She felt captured, held prisoner by that gaze in the best of ways.

"I think it's almost time to get out of here," Sammi said, her voice quiet and a little gravelly. Super sexy. Hot. Sent a pleasant little flutter low in Keegan's body and a surge of wetness to her underwear. She had to clear her throat to find her voice.

"I'm ready when you are."

Sammi leaned close. "Honey, I've been ready for days. Weeks, even. I mean, probably months."

"Okay," Keegan said, lowering her voice to match Sammi's near whisper. "That did things to me. Let's go."

It was just after eleven. They said their good-byes in record time, though Sammi did linger in a hug with her mom, and Keegan thought the beginning of each new year must mean feeling farther and farther away from the life they'd had with Sammi's dad.

"You okay?" she asked, once they were outside, Sammi leading her across the street by the hand.

"I am. New Year's Eve is rough on my mom sometimes. I wish she'd find someone."

"She will." They trudged through the new snow that had fallen earlier that day. "It just takes time to find someone who makes you feel the way you want to feel."

Sammi nodded as she slid her key into the lock, then pushed the door open. They were immediately greeted by Beckett, who was so excited to see them, it was like they'd been gone for years instead of hours. Sammi got down on the floor with him the second she'd stepped out of her boots to love on him and remind him who was the goodest boy. It was adorable to watch.

Keegan took her coat and boots off while Sammi and Beckett bounded through the house to the back door.

Tonight was the night.

She knew it. She could feel it. Yes, they'd left the Sorensons' house early so they could kiss at midnight and not feel like they were on display to all the older folks that were rooting for them, but there was going to be more. Keegan didn't plan on going home until tomorrow, unless Sammi had other ideas, which she was pretty sure she didn't.

And then Sammi and Beckett were back inside, and Sammi's face was…

"You're glowing," Keegan said to her, amused.

"Of course I am," was Sammi's reply. "Everything I want tonight is right here in my house. Why wouldn't I glow?"

"Everything you want?" Keegan asked as Sammi stepped closer.

"Everything." One more step put Sammi in her space, breathing her air. Sammi tipped her face up slightly and her lips met Keegan's, and they kissed softly.

When they parted a bit, Keegan whispered, "It's not midnight yet."

"I don't care," Sammi said. "I've been wanting to kiss you all night."

"Well then, by all means…" And she leaned down and kissed Sammi again, deepened it this time. And goddamn, Sammi was a good kisser. She knew this, knew it and remembered it from last year, from last week even, but this felt like a whole new level of sexy, as if her brain had downplayed how good it had been to protect her heart. And now? It came crashing back…the joy of kissing Sammi, the contentedness she felt just being near her, the absolute bliss of physical contact with her. It was almost overwhelming. In a good way. In a sexy, amazing way. "I think we should take this upstairs," she said, looking Sammi in the eye.

"I couldn't agree more."

They headed up the stairs.

Keegan had never been in Sammi's bedroom, a fact she realized with surprise as she entered. It was lovely, all deep greens and ivories, and felt warm and inviting, like a forest sanctuary. The bed was neatly made, covered with soft-looking pillows and a thick comforter. Keegan thought it looked like an incredibly comfortable place to read, watch TV, do other things...

That was about all she had time to think about before Sammi was kissing her again, her hands holding Keegan's face while her mouth explored, and then hands slipped into her hair and tugged, exposing her neck to the onslaught of Sammi's tongue, her lips, her warmth.

Her heart rate had kicked up, and a soft moan escaped her before she could catch it.

Sammi pulled back slightly and met her eyes. "Okay?" she asked softly.

In response, Keegan leaned back into the kiss, pulling a small chuckle from Sammi.

This woman.

Those two words ran through her head so many times.

This woman.

What had she been so scared of? Yes, the feelings were there, and they were surging just like the last time, but she felt different tonight. Instead of shoving them away, instead of trying to ignore them or put them in a box for later, she let them surge, let them come, let them wash over her like waves, like her mom had suggested. And rather than the flood of the tsunami she'd feared that last time, they were like gentle lapping waves of the ocean, warm and soothing and peaceful.

Clothes came off quickly and without preamble, and then they were on the bed naked, lying on their sides and facing each other. Sammi stroked her hair off her forehead, then followed the strands with her fingertips, toying with it.

"You are so beautiful," Sammi said quietly, her voice almost reverent. "Do you know that?"

"I'm so glad you think so," she said, then moved closer so she could press their lips together once more.

Kissing Sammi.

God, how to describe the feeling. She flashed back again to

the last time, how the way Sammi kissed her, how the way it made her feel had rushed through her like an alarm. It was that good. It was that intense. And it hadn't changed. Sammi's mouth, her lips, her tongue—God, her tongue—all worked together, especially once Sammi left her mouth and began to trail down her neck, across her collarbone, and down to her breasts. When she closed her mouth on a nipple, Keegan moaned, long and deep.

Sammi pulled back for a second and looked at her with expectantly raised eyebrows.

Keegan laughed softly. "I'm good. I'm good. Promise." She pulled Sammi's head back to her chest and let herself get lost in the sensations for a moment, but her mind kept bringing her back to Sammi's hesitation. She understood it, knew Sammi was likely flashing back as often as she was and was probably worried about the same thing happening.

She made a decision right then.

She took over.

Rolled them so Sammi was suddenly underneath her. She could tell by Sammi's wide eyes that she'd surprised her, and something about that sent a surge of sensuality through her, a zap of eroticism that she liked. A lot.

"What?" she said, looking down at Sammi's face, which had gone from surprised to...something hot. Sexy. "I don't want you worrying about me."

"I mean, I'm gonna wor—" She cut off Sammi's words with a searing kiss that, when they finally parted, left them both breathing raggedly. "Okay," Sammi said, breathless.

Keegan took Sammi's hand and placed it on her chest, over her heart. She held it there with her own hand as she asked, "Feel that?" It was racing, very easy to pick up with the simple palm of her hand, and Keegan could actually feel it in her neck, her head, her ears. At Sammi's nod, she whispered, "That's what you do to me."

"Yeah?"

"Yeah. So stop worrying."

"Okay," Sammi whispered. And it instantly became clear that

she *did* stop worrying because Sammi went all in on her body. All. In. Keegan tried to maintain the control she'd swiped, but her words to Sammi had done something. Something insanely sexy. They'd opened a seal or cracked a vault and unleashed a truly erotic version of Samantha Sorenson that Keegan had never expected, let alone seen. Sammi was gentle, yet firm. Tender, yet hard. Giving, yet demanding. Keegan had never been with someone so intently focused on her body, on her pleasure, and she came twice before she finally grasped Sammi's hand, looked her in the eye, and said firmly, "My turn."

Sammi's eyes hooded and darkened, and she gave one nod, then let Keegan shift them so she was on top once more.

Keegan did her best to go slow, but goddamn, it was hard. She'd known Sammi's body was going to be attractive, but she didn't expect it to be as fit and firm and rounded and soft and curved as it was. Her skin was hot and velvety and smelled like nutmeg. Her breasts were more ample than she'd expected, a pleasant surprise that she took advantage of, spending extra time on them, using her teeth to draw out sexy little gasps. Sammi's hands were in her hair, and she could feel her fingers clenching and unclenching as she worshipped her breasts.

Finally, she made her way down Sammi's torso, kissing her ribs, her stomach, running her tongue along her sides, until she pushed up to her knees and drew Sammi's legs slowly apart. Their eyes met and held, Keegan's hands on Sammi's knees, Sammi's hands gripping the sheets on either side of her. Neither of them said a thing, but it felt like an entire conversation about trust and consent and deeper feelings than they were ready to voice took place. And making sure not to lose eye contact, Keegan lowered herself to Sammi's center, still watching her face as she used the very tip of her tongue to touch the hot, wet, swollen flesh there.

Sammi's eyes drifted closed, and she let out a long, soft groan, and Keegan focused her concentration.

❖

Sammi's phone said it was going on three in the morning. She should be dead asleep, thanks to the workout she and Keegan had given each other, but instead, she was wide awake, her mind racing as it replayed all that had happened in the previous few hours.

Keegan lay sleeping next to her, her breathing deep and even. She was so achingly beautiful that Sammi had a hard time with her own breath, finding it catching in her throat on a regular basis at the sight next to her.

Keegan was on her back. One knee was bent so her legs made a figure four, and her foot was out from under the covers. Amusing, as it was about twenty degrees outside. She was still naked, her bare shoulders visible, even as the blankets covered what had turned out to be the most gorgeous breasts Sammi had ever had the privilege of seeing, touching, tasting. One arm was bent, her hand in a loose fist against her temple, her auburn hair spread out over the pillow.

Sammi watched her breathe.

A small part of her chuckled internally over how stalkerish it was to watch somebody sleep. But the rest of her was enamored. She flashed back to the sounds Keegan made, the moans, the soft whimpers that built up to her orgasm—not loud, but definitely... exuberant. Sammi smiled in the dim light of the room as she recalled that beautiful sound, part gasp, part cry, all sexy.

Beckett made a snorfling sound from his big dog bed in the corner. He'd been making it a habit to sleep on the bed with Sammi, but there'd clearly been too much activity for him tonight, and he'd adjourned to his bed, which had made her and Keegan laugh in relief.

Now, he was clearly dreaming about something. When Sammi peeked over the edge of the bed at him, his legs were twitching like he was running in his sleep.

Deciding she didn't like that everybody was sleeping except her, she snuggled down into the covers and laid her head on the pillow next to Keegan, who sighed softly in her sleep and then, to Sammi's surprise, opened her eyes and smiled.

"Were you going to watch me sleep all night?" she whispered with a grin.

Sammi felt her cheeks heat up. "Too creepy?"

"Not at all."

It was dark, but they held gazes. Sammi could make out the clearness of Keegan's eyes, the light color. When she spoke, it was very, very softly. "I never expected to be here. Like this. With you."

"And yet here we are."

"Here we are." A beat passed. "And you're okay?"

Keegan's smile was tender. "I really, really am." Sammi smiled and closed her eyes, but Keegan's hand was on her face. "Hey. Look at me." Sammi did. "There is nowhere—*nowhere*—I'd rather be right now than in your bed with you."

Maybe it was the warmth of Keegan's palm against her cheek. Maybe it was the intensity of her eye contact. Maybe it was the tone of her voice. But something finally washed relief through Sammi's bloodstream like an injection. It rushed through her brain, through her heart, and just like that, her worry evaporated, and her eyes welled up the smallest bit.

She cleared her throat. "Well. What a coincidence. I feel the same way."

"Good. Then you should probably kiss me."

Sammi did as she was told.

CHAPTER SIXTEEN

A fresh start.

That's what today was.

That's how Keegan always looked at the early morning hours of New Year's Day. It didn't matter what mistakes you'd made in the past because you could toss them away and start fresh. This was her chance to begin again. And that's what she was doing. She was starting fresh. With Sammi.

Of course, Sammi probably didn't know that yet, had zero idea. But Keegan did. She'd known that moment in the middle of the night when Sammi's eyes had filled with unshed tears. She'd kept them under control, hadn't let them fall, but the fact that they'd shown up at all was the only thing Keegan needed to understand exactly how Sammi felt about her.

It was the same way Keegan felt about Sammi.

She loved her.

As if those unshed tears had unlocked some kind of gate, it swung open, and the feelings for Sammi she'd been burying, fighting, denying all came rushing out like her kindergarteners when the dismissal bell released them into the sunlight.

She stood now in Sammi's kitchen, watching out the window as Beckett bounded through the snow, sticking his nose in it, then tossing his head so the snow flew through the air. He was having the time of his doggie life, and she couldn't help but smile at him. Bringing him home to Sammi was probably one of the most enjoyable things she'd ever done in her life. Watching Sammi's face light up and her eyes fill with love for the dog that Keegan had known the very first time she'd seen them together was a dog made for Sammi was one of the most gorgeous, joyful moments she'd ever experienced.

Beckett had woken bright and early, and Keegan knew that Sammi had been awake much of the night—well, so had she, but Sammi had been awake longer—so she was letting her sleep a bit. She'd quietly snuck out of the bedroom with Beckett by her side and closed the door behind them.

The coffee was strong and rich this morning. Maybe because of that whole fresh start thing? She smiled at the silliness of the thought as she opened the back door to let Beckett in. He was still pretty full of energy and she didn't want him to wake up Sammi yet, so she got one of his tug toys out and sat on the living room floor with it.

Beckett was not a small dog, and he was decidedly strong, but he seemed to go easy on her.

"Are you letting me win?" she asked him as she tugged on the rope with both hands. "Pretty sure you could drag me across the room."

Beckett's nubby tail kept wagging and he held the rope firmly in his teeth. Every few seconds, he'd stop and rest—still holding the rope—and then he'd pull some more.

"So, Becks," she said to him as they played. "What should I do? I could use some advice."

The dog didn't let go of the rope, but he stopped tugging and stared at her with his sweet brown eyes as if he was listening and saying *Go on*.

"So, here's the thing…" She swallowed hard, because this subject was scary enough just being in her head. And yes, she was talking to a dog, but she was still saying these things out loud, and that made them even scarier. "I think I love your mom." She blew out a short breath of relief. "I mean, I know I love her. Everybody does. How could you not, right? She's amazing. But…" And here, she took another moment or two to brace herself before saying, very quietly, "I think I'm *in love* with her."

Beckett continued to watch her, his eye contact almost intimidatingly intense.

"And I don't know if I should tell her. 'Cause it's fast. Really fast. The last time we were together—this was before we knew you—I hurt her pretty badly. So I'm not sure if she feels the same way for me any longer. You know? I mean, I think she does…" She sighed and looked at the floor, remembering her thoughts from earlier and that moment last night when Sammi had nearly cried. "No. I know she does."

"She absolutely does."

Keegan gasped and spun herself on the floor to see Sammi standing in the doorway from the steps. Beckett abandoned the game of tug and ran to his person, so happy to see her. He jumped up and put his front paws on Sammi's hip, and Sammi petted his head, but her eyes never left Keegan's.

"She absolutely does," she said again.

It was Keegan's turn to have her eyes well up, but she wasn't able to keep the tears from spilling over. "Yeah?"

"Oh, don't cry. Come here." Sammi opened her arms so Keegan could stand up and walk into them, which was exactly what she did. Sammi smelled like warmth and sleep and love, and Keegan inhaled deeply as she buried her face in that spot where Sammi's neck met her shoulder. "I have loved you from the minute we had our first date, and I never stopped loving you throughout the past year."

Keegan looked up at her with surprise. "Seriously?"

Sammi nodded and said, "Even when you were dating *Jules*." She pretended to choke on the name, which made Keegan laugh and broke any tension that had filtered into the room. They held each other for another moment and Sammi said, "I want to ask you how you didn't notice, but I think I did a commendable job of hiding it. Kinda."

"You did. Kinda." She squeezed Sammi tightly.

"Is this where we have the what-happens-now discussion?"

"We probably should." Keegan looked up at her. "What happens now?"

"Wait, no." Sammi shook her head as she whined. "I was gonna ask that."

"Yeah, but I asked first," Keegan deadpanned, then laughed.

Sammi kept an arm around her as they moved into the living room and sat down on the couch.

"Seriously, though," Keegan said, "what happens now?"

Sammi blew out a long, slow breath. "I mean, I think we...live. Right? It's the perfect day to start our life together, you and me."

"And Beckett."

"And Beckett."

"And Cocoa and Bean."

"And Cocoa and Bean."

"And your mom and grandma."

Sammi groaned and covered her eyes. "My grandma is never going to let me live this down."

"Nor should she," Keegan said with a laugh. "She's a very subtle and very good matchmaker."

"God, don't tell her that. And she's hardly subtle. She'll be pairing up people all over town."

"Hey, the world is a mess. Everybody could use a little more love."

"You are not wrong, my friend." Sammi petted Beckett's big square head.

"I love you, Sammi," Keegan said quietly.

Sammi met her eyes and smiled that gorgeous smile of hers. "I love you, too."

"Happy New Year."

"Happy New Year, baby." Sammi leaned in, and Keegan pressed her lips to the ones she wanted to kiss forever.

EPILOGUE

One year later

Mia had outdone herself with Christmas Eve dinner this year. She could admit it. She didn't even mind cooking meat for others. She just wanted her guests to be happy and full. The roast was cooked to perfection, a lovely, crusty sear on the outside while the inside remained juicy and slightly pink—only slightly or Angelo would moan and whine about it still mooing. She smiled when she thought about that, though, because Angelo had become a dear friend over the past year and was either over for dinner or invited her to dinner at least once a week. And he had brought his beau of six months now, Charles, to Christmas Eve dinner, so she wasn't going to give him too much of a hard time. He was clearly in love, and she was too happy for him to harass him. For now.

"What can I do, Mom?" Maggie came into the kitchen, rubbing her hands together as if itching for a task.

"You've been weird all day," Mia said, stopping her basting of the roast to look at her daughter-in-law. "Are you all right?"

"What? Me? Absolutely. Just excited about Christmas. Aren't you?"

"Sweetie, I'm eighty-one years old. Not much excites me anymore." She finished basting, then moved the roast to a cutting board to rest for a few minutes before she sliced it up. Hulk sat quietly off to the side, having learned if he didn't beg too vocally, the chances of him getting a bite of meat went up in a big way.

"Do you want me to slice that so you don't have to?" Maggie asked.

"I appreciate that, sweetie, but no. I'm fine. Thank you."

With a shrug, Maggie grabbed the salt and pepper and took it out to the dining room. Something was up with that one, but she didn't have time to suss it out right now.

"Oh my God, that smells amazing." Sammi came into the kitchen and kissed Mia on the cheek.

Beckett trotted in behind her, seemed to figure out what was happening, and sat down right next to Hulk. They barely greeted one another.

"Well, hello there, my girl. And my boy." She petted Beckett's head, then slipped him and Hulk each a small chunk of beef that had crisped on the pan. "Merry Christmas."

"Merry Christmas, Grams."

"You look very pretty today," Mia complimented. Sammi was dressed up nicely in black dress pants and a lightweight red sweater. She'd grown her hair out for the past several months and now had it partially pulled back, the rest cascading over her shoulders in dark waves that were the same color as her father's. Her dark eyes—also just like her dad's—were bright. Happy. It had been a good year for her. "When will Keegan get here?"

Sammi glanced at her watch. "Any time now." Her smile was wide, telling Mia she was excited and happy that Keegan was bringing her parents and sister with her to Christmas Eve dinner. "Thanks again for inviting them."

"Keegan is part of the family to me, honey."

"I'm really glad you feel that way." Sammi glanced over toward the counter where all the alcohol had been set up like a makeshift bar. "Hey, is there champagne in the fridge?"

"I think? If not, put some in it."

Sammi gave a nod, then grabbed two bottles from the counter and put them both in the refrigerator—no easy feat, since it was already packed full of Christmas food. Mia watched as Sammi found space, shoved them both in, then smiled at her and left the room just as the doorbell rang, causing a cacophony of dog barks, likely the Duffys arriving.

An hour later, everybody was seated at Mia's large dining room table and enjoying both the dinner and the company, if the smiles and laughter were any indication. These were the times she missed her Bob more than anything. Yes, it had been more than fifteen years since he'd passed, but she could still picture him sitting at the head of the table opposite her where Sammi sat now. She could still hear his laughter as he told ridiculous anecdotes Sammi called his dad jokes. She could still see him smile across the table at her, making her knees go weak well into her late sixties. Maggie had tried to get her to date after Bob died, but she hadn't seemed to understand that no other man could come close to comparing. Of course, Maggie understood it now, even as Mia pushed *her* to date. She was far too young to spend the rest of her life alone.

Keegan and her family sat at the far end of the table near Sammi, her parents on one side, Keegan and Shannon on the other. Then Maggie, Angelo, and Charles, who leaned toward each other like a troublemaking trio in high school. Every now and then, Maggie would burst out laughing, which made Mia smile because since Kevin's death, Maggie's laughter wasn't something heard often.

A clang rang out as Sammi dropped her fork. For the second time. Sammi glanced at her, her eyes wide, and Mia grinned at her, even as she wondered why she seemed so jumpy.

"Mia, this dinner is fantastic." That was Charles, Angelo's boyfriend. Mia liked him a lot. He seemed kind and polite and very attentive to Angelo. Didn't let him take himself too seriously.

"Thank you, Charles. I'm so glad you could come." She smiled at him, and his face lit up.

"It's my first holiday with people since my husband passed, so…" He blushed a bit, his cheeks turning pink beneath his neatly trimmed beard. "Thank you for inviting me."

She hadn't known that, and she softened even more toward him. "You're very welcome."

Suddenly, Sammi was up on her feet. "Champagne?" Before

anybody could answer, she hurried off to the kitchen, then came back with a bottle. Flutes had been set at each place, so she removed the cork, which came out with a fun pop, and went around the table, pouring the golden liquid into glasses, overflowing two of them.

Mia stood up and took the bottle from her, giving her a look that clearly said *What's the matter with you?* She filled the rest of the flutes as Sammi returned to her end of the table but didn't sit. She waited for Mia to finish and sit back down, and suddenly, Sammi had everybody's attention.

"Okay, so. I have a few words, if nobody minds."

Nobody did, the conversation dying down to silence as everybody's attention moved to Sammi. It wasn't unlike her to give toasts and little speeches, Mia knew. She'd actually become quite good at such things, giving both eulogies and toasts when her grandfather and then her father had passed. Mia focused on her granddaughter, who was clearly nervous, judging by the slightly trembling hand holding her champagne. That *was* unusual.

"This past year has been"—Sammi grinned and shook her head—"so many things." Her gaze traveled as she spoke. "Getting used to life with that guy." She indicated Beckett, who sat at attention in the doorway next to Hulk, neither of whom were allowed in the dining room or they'd beg and drool all over the place. "Mom found some new good friends who've been hauling her out of her shell."

"She might be on a dating app," Angelo chimed in, his hands cupped around his mouth, and a collective happy gasp went around the table.

"Mom! That's amazing," Sammi said, eyes wide.

"He said might," Maggie said, her face going deep red. "*Might*."

"Mm-hmm," was all Angelo had to say to that, and Mia reached over to grasp her daughter-in-law's hand and give it a squeeze, hoping her approval showed in her eyes when Maggie met them.

"These two," Sammi went on, indicating Angelo and Charles, "have become so very important to this family. We're so glad you found each other. And us."

Angelo leaned into Charles, whose arm was around him. Their

smiles said it all, and Mia felt her chest warm with her love for them both.

"And I've become part of what feels like a second family," Sammi went on, her gaze moving to the Duffys. "I don't want to say new family, because my own is so important to me, even as it grows. But second, definitely." Mia watched as Sammi's gaze moved from Keegan's parents to her sister to her. "And that brings me to this one." Her eyes stayed on Keegan's, and even if Mia hadn't been there from the beginning, even if she hadn't had the tiniest bit of a hand in bringing the two of them together, the love was glaringly apparent. On both their faces. She'd have seen it even if she'd walked into this house for the very first time and had just met them. "You," Sammi went on, "are the most incredible, giving, loving woman I have ever met. Every morning when I open my eyes, the first thing I do is reach for you. And if it's one of those rare days where you had to stay at your place or I had to stay at mine, I search my brain to make sure we're really a thing and not some wonderful dream I had in the night."

Keegan smiled at her, her eyes soft and bright and filled with love for Mia's granddaughter. "We're really a thing. Promise."

"Good. But I don't want to have to do that anymore," Sammi said, and Mia watched as Keegan's eyes went slightly wide, and a soft gasp went around the table as people figured out what was about to happen. Sammi set down her flute, pulled out a small velvet box, and dropped to one knee.

"Oh my God," said Keegan's mom.

"Keegan Elizabeth Duffy," Sammi said, tears clear in her eyes and voice, even from the other end of the table where Mia sat, "I love you so very much. Will you make it so that I never have to wonder again and be my wife?"

Keegan was nodding vigorously even before Sammi had finished her question, and she almost stepped on Sammi's lines with her own very exuberant, "Yes!" She threw herself into Sammi's arms as the entire table erupted into cheers and applause, Mia included. She'd never been happier in her life, and she clapped loudly as her eyes filled with tears of happiness.

Keegan pulled Sammi to her feet, and they kissed and hugged and murmured words of love to each other. Mia glanced at Maggie, who didn't look terribly surprised, and the pieces fell into place.

"You knew," Mia said on a gasp, then laughed as she playfully shoved at her daughter-in-law.

Maggie's poker face had always been nonexistent, and she glanced down guiltily. But before she could confirm or deny or offer an excuse, Sammi spoke up.

"She did, Grams, but there was a reason for that." The table went quiet as all eyes turned to Sammi. "It was because I wanted to run something by her first."

Mia was thoroughly confused now, and trying not to feel a bit hurt that Sammi hadn't let her in on her plans. It must have shown on her face, because Sammi smiled at her as she came around the table and held her hands out to Mia. Mia took them, and Sammi pulled her to her feet.

"Grandma, you have always been my rock. My conscience, my voice of reason, my favorite person on the planet. No offense, Mom."

Maggie laughed. "None taken."

"So, I was wondering..." Sammi swallowed hard and her dark eyes, so much like Kevin's, pooled with tears. "Would you be my best man? Err...woman? Err...person?" She sighed. "Would you stand up with me at my wedding?"

Mia blinked at her, speechless—something that didn't happen to Mia Sorenson. Ever. But this? This was...it was so many things. Unexpected. An honor. A privilege. Unheard of. She blinked some more until Sammi gave their still-linked hands a little shake.

"Grams?"

Mia cleared her throat, trying to stave off her own tears at least for another moment or two. "Well, that's the silliest question I've ever heard." And just as Sammi's face was about to fall, she added, "Of course I will. You don't even have to ask. I will be the *best* best person you've ever seen." She reached her hand up and laid her palm against Sammi's cheek. "*Of course I will.*"

And then they were hugging, and the guests erupted again

into applause and cheers and hugs. Keegan's parents hugged, then hauled Shannon into their midst. Angelo and Charles had their arms around each other and clasped Maggie's hand across the table. Then Maggie came around and wrapped up Sammi, and Keegan was suddenly there, hugging Mia. Even Beckett and Hulk were not to be left out of the celebration, breaking the rules and bounding into the room to push into Sammi with vigor and love.

God, had there ever been a room filled with such love before?

Mia simply watched in awe and happiness until Sammi put a champagne flute back in her hand and picked up her own, held it aloft until the rest of the room followed and quieted.

"I'd like to propose a toast. To Mia Sorenson. The best volunteer, mother-in-law, and grandmother in the world." She met Mia's eyes. "And matchmaker extraordinaire. Thank you, Grams. And Merry Christmas. You're stuck with all of us now, and we love you."

Mia's tears wouldn't stay in her eyes this time. They spilled over and tracked down her cheeks as she looked around the table at all her guests. Her *family*. "I love you all, and I wouldn't have it any other way," she said, and she held up her own glass. "Merry Christmas."

About the Author

Georgia Beers lives in Upstate New York and has written more than thirty-five novels of sapphic romance. In her off-hours, she can usually be found searching for a scary movie, sipping a good Pinot, or trying to keep up with little big man Archie, her mix of many little dogs. Find out more at georgiabeers.com.

Books Available From Bold Strokes Books

Accidentally in Love by Kimberly Cooper Griffin. Nic and Lee have good reasons for keeping their distance. So why does their growing attraction seem more like a love-hate relationship? (978-1-63679-759-5)

Frosted by the Girl Next Door by Aurora Rey and Jaime Clevenger. When heartbroken Casey Stevens opens a sex shop next door to uptight cupcake baker Tara McCoy, things get a little frosty. (978-1-63679-723-6)

Ghost of the Heart by Catherine Friend. Being possessed by a ghost was not on Gwen's bucket list, but she must admit that ghosts might be real, and one is obviously trying to send her a message. (978-1-63555-112-9)

Hot Honey Love by Nan Campbell. When chef Stef Lombardozzi puts her cooking career into the hands of filmmaker Mallory Radowski—the pickiest eater alive—she doesn't anticipate how hard she'll fall for her. (978-1-63679-743-4)

London by Patricia Evans. Jaq's and Bronwyn's lives become entwined as dangerous secrets emerge and Bronwyn's seemingly perfect life starts to unravel. (978-1-63679-778-6)

This Christmas by Georgia Beers. When Sam's grandmother rigs the Christmas parade to make Sam and Keegan queen and queen, sparks fly, but they can't forget the Big Embarrassing Thing that makes romance a total nope. (978-1-63679-729-8)

Unwrapped by D. Jackson Leigh. Asia du Muir is not going to let some party-girl actress ruin her best chance to get noticed by a Broadway critic. Everyone knows you should never mix business and pleasure. (978-1-63679-667-3)

The First Kiss by Patricia Evans. As the intrigue surrounding her latest case spins dangerously out of control, military police detective Parker

Haven must choose between her career and the woman she's falling in love with. (978-1-63679-775-5)

Language Lessons by Sage Donnell. Grace and Lenka never expected to fall in love. Is home really where the heart is if it means giving up your dreams? (978-1-63679-725-0)

New Horizons by Shia Woods. When Quinn Collins meets Alex Anders, Horizon Theater's enigmatic managing director, a passionate connection ignites, but amidst the complex backdrop of theater politics, their budding romance faces a formidable challenge. (978-1-63679-683-3)

Scrambled: A Tuesday Night Book Club Mystery by Jaime Maddox. Avery Hutchins makes a discovery about her father's death that will force her to face an impossible choice between doing what is right and finally finding a way to regain a part of herself she had lost. (978-1-63679-703-8)

Stolen Hearts by Michele Castleman. Finding the thief who stole a precious heirloom will become Ella's first move in a dangerous game of wits that exposes family secrets and could lead to her family's financial ruin. (978-1-63679-733-5)

Synchronicity by J.J. Hale. Dance, destiny, and undeniable passion collide at a summer camp as Haley and Cal navigate a love story that intertwines past scars with present desires. (978-1-63679-677-2)

Wild Fire by Radclyffe & Julie Cannon. When Olivia returns to the Red Sky Ranch, Riley's carefully crafted safe world goes up in flames. Can they take a risk and cross the fire line to find love? (978-1-63679-727-4)

Writ of Love by Cassidy Crane. Kelly and Jillian struggle to navigate the ruthless battleground of Big Law, grappling with desire, ambition, and the thin line between success and surrender. (978-1-63679-738-0)